Anna J. Terrot

Scenes from the Life of the First Benedictines

Anna J. Terrot

Scenes from the Life of the First Benedictines

ISBN/EAN: 9783337376932

Printed in Europe, USA, Canada, Australia, Japan

Cover: Foto ©Andreas Hilbeck / pixelio.de

More available books at **www.hansebooks.com**

SCENES

FROM THE LIFE OF

THE

FIRST BENEDICTINES.

DEDICATED TO

DR. PUSEY, D.D.

London:

REMINGTON AND CO.,

5, ARUNDEL STREET, STRAND, W.C

1877.

PREFACE.

THERE can scarcely be a grander subject for contemplation than the life of the early Benedictines, with its glorification of humility, labour, and obedience ; and in its voluntary pauperism, rapt asceticism, and radiant happiness. I have clothed, whenever it was possible (thanks to a good memory), the thoughts which this subject gave rise to, in the words of our poets. But when I could not remember, or they did not express the ideas suggested, I was obliged to use my own words.

The proceeds of this little work, if any, are to be devoted to the relief of the sick poor in Spitalfields and Bethnal Green.

ANNA J. TERROT,

English Sister of Charity.

PERSONS REPRESENTED.

Eutropius.

Benedict (Abbot).

Scholastique (Abbess).

Margaret.

Bouverie.

Romanus.

Clare.

Adèle.

Angela.

Agnes.

Grace.

Euphemia.

Lucy.

Constance.

Augusta.

Dora.

Jane.

Angels, &c.

Maur (Assistant-Superior and Master of Novices).

Bernard (S. Benedict's Guardian-Angel in the Habit of a Monk).

Sylvester.

Placidus.

Fitzroi.

George.

Evangeline.

Claude.

Dunstan.

Cuthbert.

William } Christian Martyrs.
Richard }

Vincent.

Victor.

Lucian (Penitent-Angel in the Habit of a Monk.)

Ambrose.

Sebastian.

James.

&c., &c.

SCENES FROM THE LIFE OF THE FIRST BENEDICTINES.

SCENE 1.

A Room in the Castle of Lord Eutropius.—Enter EUTROPIUS, SCHOLASTIQUE, *and* MARGARET. SCHOLASTIQUE *in Nun's apparel.*

EUTROPIUS—Father Bouverie says the vow your
    mother made, may be revoked.*
The final choice is yours ; let it content you
    then
To be your cousin's wife : I know you love
    him well.
SCHOLASTIQUE—Thro' him I've touch'd the
    height of human happiness,
To find there was a heaven beyond it ;

---

* Scholastique was vowed by her mother to the religious life as soon
as she was born.

B

But now I hate myself for that I lov'd,
And doted more on him than on my GOD.
MARGARET—My Lord Eutropius, do persuade
    her if your can.

> [*Clings to* SCHOLASTIQUE.

Do not be shorn a nun, and leave us all.
SCHOLASTIQUE—Ah ! Margaret when the har-
    mony of heaven
Soundeth the measure of a lively faith,
The sweetest music of this world
Is odious, tuneless, and most wearisome:
O ! would to GOD that you might learn of me,
To seek heaven's joy before earth's vanity.

> [MARGARET *weeps.*

Why do you weep ?
Is not heaven's joy before earth's fading bliss,
And life above sweeter than life in love ?
Farewell to friends and father ! welcome
    CHRIST !
Adieu to dainty robes ! this coarse attire
Better befits an humble mind to GOD,
Than all the show of rich habiliments.

I leave both love, and love's content at once,
Betaking me to Him that is true love,
And leaving all the world for love of Him.
                    [*Exeunt* SCHOLASTIQUE *and* MARGARET.
EUTROPIUS—I dare not stay thee, if thou be
    so fixed:
Shall I regret to see thee so near GOD?
Nay, GOD forbid! Sweet sacrifice
'On which e'en heaven itself throws incense!
                    [*Enter* FATHER BOUVERIE.
BOUVERIE—My Lord Eutropius, has your ward
    fixed the day?
EUTROPIUS—Father, not yet; I wish she would,
    For her own sake, as well as Benedict's.
BOUVERIE—He's grown a very handsome
    youth.
EUTROPIUS—He has such noble shape, so soft a
    grace,
So full of worth withal, that every maid
That looks upon him, gives away herself
To him for ever; but he has fixed
His eye, not to be moved, on Margaret—

BOUVERIE—And she?

EUTROPIUS—Mere *in love* is poor expression of
      her doting,

   And she's in nothing happier than in knowing
   It is returned by him.

BOUVERIE—Well, GOD bless them! a lovelier
      couple

   Sure I'll never join, I'm on my way

   To see Romanus. Will you come with me?

EUTROPIUS—I've often heard of that strange
      man,

   But never seen him yet; what is he like?

BOUVERIE—He's shrouded in a strait sack of
      most harsh texture, girded with a knotted
      cord.

   A large, coarse, pyramidal hood drawn over
      the head down to the eyes;

   A streaming beard, the visage half-swallowed
      up in that gloomy grove,

   The eyes sunk as if fearfully retiring from
      profane objects, and silently imploring:

   Keep us Lord, from the vanities of the world!

EUTROPIUS—Our village was last evening almost
    empty,
And I was told that all had gone to hear
    Romanus preach.
BOUVERIE—I went with the crowd : a rude
    pulpit was erected close to his hermit cell.
He entered it with CHRIST in hand, and Hell
    before his face ;
And from the thicket of that penitential
    beard,
Came burning words, ploughing up men's
    hearts.
EUTROPIUS—What did he preach upon ?
BOUVERIE—The Day of Judgment, and the End-
    less Tragedy ;
And with such tremendous power,
That he filled even the most insensible
With terror and dismay ; and frequently
Was he interrupted by the wailings,
And the sobs of his hearers, with whose tears
Romanus silent for a space, did mix his own.
EUTROPIUS—You raise my interest.

BOUVERIE—Then come and see the man.

EUTROPIUS—I will.

[Exeunt.

SCENE 2.

MARGARET *and* BENEDICT *walking in the grounds of the Castle—Church in sight—attended by their guardian angels.*

MARGARET—A most strict house; a house
    where none may whisper,
Where no more light is known, but what
    may make you believe there is a day.

BENEDICT—Believe not such reports:
    My Sister's nuns are young and healthy,
    And enjoy light and air as much as you:
    The rule is strict, not stricter than they wish.

MARGARET—I do rejoice to hear it.
    How fast this hour has gone;
    See! those that have been offering Evensong,
    Are now returning homeward:
    I must be gone—

BENEDICT—You shall not leave me thus :
  Come, join your hands to mine, your heart
    is mine,
  Confirm it with an oath.
MARGARET—You do wrong us both :
  People hereafter shall not say, there pass'd
    a bond, more than our loves, to tie
    our lives,
  And deaths together.
BENEDICT—It is as nobly said as I would wish.
MARGARET—Again farewell! a good night to you.
BENEDICT—Lock up those sweet lights in pleas-
    ing slumbers :
  All the dear joys here, above, hereafter,
  Crown thy fair soul!

                    [He kisses her.
BENEDICT'S GUARDIAN—The last kiss, for GOD
    has other work for you :
  I've sworn to bring thee to the highest life,
  And here, by all things sacred, do again.
MARGARET'S GUARDIAN—And Margaret too, she's
    called

To higher things she knows not yet:
Seeds must have time to sprout, before they
spring.

[Exeunt.

SCENE 3.

A Room in the Castle—Enter EUTROPIUS *and*
BENEDICT.

BENEDICT.—What! marry Lady Margaret
After such a vision! again must I declare it—
I saw the Stigmata as plainly as I see you
now.

[Clasps his hands.

O! Mystery of Love!
In which absorbed, anguish, despair of self,
And loss of all this world most precious
holds,
Only enlarged my rapture.
Shall I refuse obedience to the call of such a
GOD!

Because the world, the devil, and the flesh,
My father also, try to drag me back?
By Heaven, I would as soon forsake my
    standard,
When the full tide of battle beats against it,
And like a recreant, fly to join the foe!
    [EUTROPIUS *waving his hand deprecatingly.*
Well, well, I'll say no more:
What do you mean to do?
BENEDICT—In the neighb'ring district
There lives an holy man, whose sanctity
Is marked with wondrous gifts;
Grace smiles upon him;
Conversion tracks his footsteps; miracles
Spring from his touch; his sacred casuistry
Pours balm into despair: I will consult with
    him.
EUTROPIUS—You mean that blessed anchorite,
    Romanus?
BENEDICT—I do.
EUTROPIUS—Then GOD's will must be done.
    Heaven! you weep—

BENEDICT—It is that speaking likeness,
        [*Looks up at his mother's picture.**
Which has filled mine eyes with tears ;
Foolish that I am to let it do so.
EUTROPIUS (*aside*)—Sweet and noble nature !
    (*Aloud*)—Farewell, my Benedict : never, never
Shall I taste fruit of all the worldly hopes
I had in thee.   Precious to me, the thought
Of thy delightful infancy ; when first
Returning from the wars, my boy †
Would kiss his father in his burganet,
And, viewing the bright metal, smile to see
Another little Benet smile on thee ;
And when my wounds have smarted, I have
        sung
With an unskilful, yet a willing voice,
To bring my boy asleep.   Well did I hope
That I should live to see you the world's
        wonder,

---

* Benedict was a little child when his mother died, but he never
forgot her.
    † A great portion of the life of Lord Eutropius was spent in
fighting against his country's enemies, the Goths.

So happy, great, and good, that none were
    like you :
While I, from busy life and care set free,   .
Had spent the evening of my age at home,
Among a little prattling race of yours !
There, like an old man, talked awhile; and
    then
Lain down and slept in peace . . . . . O !
    Benedict !
                   [*Embraces him.*
Pray turn from me—there's such a weight
    upon my heart . . . . all that I can
    is spoken.
              [*Sinks back in his chair.*
BENEDICT (*kneeling before him*)—Beloved father !
    never more loved than now :
Heaven shall restore the joys I have bereft you,
With full increase hereafter !
         [*Kisses his father's hand and exit.*

SCENE 4.

A Wilderness.—ROMANUS *and* BENEDICT.

BENEDICT—Dead ! did you say ?

ROMANUS—And he died well :

 He sent his love to you, Scholastique, and
  Margaret ;
 And said, " Blest be the time, that I had leave
 To call such virtue mine.
 The best of my well-being consists in theirs ;
 May they be happier than they know to wish !
 Bless them, and tell them, I cannot want
 What they are pleased to wish me."

BENEDICT—Would 'twere so, for then there is
 No blessing that can make the kindest
 And the noblest man complete,
 But should fall on him.
 Dead—Romanus—oh—I had a father,
 Whose memory I bow to ! My father !
 The very reverence of the word comes 'cross
  me

Like sacred charm. Father, as low as this
    I bow to you;   [*Kneels.*
And should as low as to your grave, to show
    a mind
Thankful for all your love.
Oh, pardon me, dear father, for all the idle and
Unreverend words that I have spoke in idle
Moods to you ! canst Thou forgive me . . .
    GOD—
When the full heart breaks thus . . . thus—
              [*Covers his face and weeps.*
ROMANUS (*after a pause*)—There is no cause to
    grieve for him.
Peace rest with him !
But now attend, I have a message
Sent to thee from GOD.
Thou art to be the head of all the Western
    Monks ;
And thou must write a rule for their guidance.
BENEDICT—Thou speakest riddles.
ROMANUS—I speak the truth: the day wears
    fast,

Come on; (*they walk*) after a short sojourn in
    the desert
You are to take your place as Abbot;
A mighty throng is waiting to hail you, "Father
Of the monastic life!" and I as nothing am
Compared to thee : and now I leave you
With the angels. [*Leads him into a rocky cavern.*
Your cell 'tis brother; where instead of masks,
Music, tilts, tourneys, and such court-like
    shows,
The hollow murmur of the checkless winds
Shall groan and moan; whilst the unquiet sea
Shakes the whole rock with foamy battery :
Here usherless the air comes in and out.
BENEDICT—It is too good.
ROMANUS—Farewell ! and when we meet again,
My will most freely I'll to you resign,
I'll be your pupil then, that once were mine.
                         [*Exit.*

BENEDICT—Bless'd spirit of my father,
O, in what orb soe'er thy soul is thron'd,
Behold me worthily most happy,

Bound by a solemn vow 'fore GOD and man
To the Religious Life.　　　　[*He kneels.*

SCENE 5.

Convent of the Sacred Heart—The Parlour.—Enter
SCHOLASTIQUE *and* MARGARET.

MARGARET—I've thrown my weaknesses before
　　your feet
To look at, touch, discourse upon, discuss :
O, then let pity hold the light of truth
Back, nor break suddenly my dream of bliss ;
For fragile is the vase containing one
Poor simple flower* dipt in it by yourself,
And if you saw it broken at your feet,
You might weep too, ere you could turn away :
Then never say that he has ceased to love me.
SCHOLASTIQUE—These were my words; "he must
　　not marry thee."

* Scholastique before she knew of God's intentions towards Benedict, encouraged the attachment between him and Lady Margaret.

Not he has ceased to love.   [*Caressing her.*
Could I have told thee had he ceased to love ?
I could as soon have crushed away the life
From a sick dove.   I did wish once that
You should be his wife : how can I now—
When God has sent him such a wondrous call
To the Religious Life ?
MARGARET—Heaven has decreed it then—
What will I do with my estates without
His love ? they'll serve me for no use
But to be buried in.   O my beloved—
                    [*Weeps. Turns to* SCHOLASTIQUE.
Help me !
O, help to stem the ebbing sea of weary life !
                    [*She weeps passionately.*
SCHOLASTIQUE—Help you, I will—to my lips
        lift my Blessed LORD (*kisses Crucifix*),
        and call His name in witness. (*Grasping*
        MARGARET) Come then . . . resist not,
Think not, hang not back . . .
Along with me ! There is no other way
To give him freedom, and thyself full peace.

MARGARET—Cling I must to somewhat : Let me
    love GOD,
Alone . . . . if it must be so !
SCHOLASTIQUE—Him alone.
    Mind, in Him only place thy trust henceforth.
    Thy hands are marble, Margaret! and thy eyes
    Are sad and soft, as are the wintry stars
    In their clear brightness.
    Blessed are they who walk in innocence,
    With the Pure, the Consecrated, the Resigned,
    And fear the LORD, and only know His saints,
    And only do His will! the arts of hell,
    The powers of darkness, be they far from thee,
    From thee, my child! she falls upon my
        knees . . . .
    She faints—help! there . . . .
[*Enter Nuns who busy themselves to recover* MAR-
        GARET.
SCHOLASTIQUE—Look on her Mary, with an
        eye of pity;
    How like the ghost of what she late appear'd,
    She lies before thee ! be a queen

In sweetness as in power; and raise her up
   to comfort.
(*To the Nuns*) O, softly set her down :
'Tis past ! she opens her sweet eyes : Sisters
   go—'tis best,
And in my loving bosom let her rest.
                     [*Exeunt Nuns.*

SCENE 6.

BENEDICT *and* SCHOLASTIQUE *walking in the
Garden of the Sacred Heart.*

BENEDICT—And what else did she say ?
SCHOLASTIQUE—I asked her how such calmness
   could proceed from her :
And she replied, "'Tis the Saints that make
   me so.
And sure my love for Benedict
Will be the nobler and the better blest,
· In that the secret anguish of the soul
Is mingled with it," and as she spoke,

Her eye did seem to labour with a tear,
Which suddenly took birth, but overweigh'd
With its own swelling, dropp'd upon her bosom.
I let her be Professed at once; I could not
    keep her back.
To me it seems, her glowing thoughts will put
Her past her meat and sleep with ecstasy;
She almost keeps the fasts of Seraphim,
And wakes for joy, like nightingale in May.
BENEDICT—My precious pearl!
We'll meet again at the great gate of Paradise,
And silence shall be up in heaven
To hear our greeting.
SCHOLASTIQUE—How beautiful she looked
, The day she was Professed! I thought that as
I saw her from the holy Altar rise,
With such a gleam of glory in her eyes,
That she might win the glance
Of any Seraph gazing not on GOD.
BENEDICT—Well, I must go 'ere the Angelus
    sounds.
SCHOLASTIQUE—Where is your Monastery?

BENEDICT—Not far from here : 'tis built upon a
    rock ;
And stands unreach'd by the rough surges ;
We only hear their hollow roar below.
SCHOLASTIQUE—And this Convent of the Sacred
    Heart
Is in a vale, half-hid by trees.
Benedict, thou wast born still to excel me ;
Thou like the eagle on some awful rock
Sublime among the clouds, thine eyrie hang'st,
From thence to soar around, with equal wing,
Through winter's storms, and summer's
    burning blaze :
I to the valley bend my feeble flight,
There in the wild wood sing my notes of praise,
Till from the spray I drop to sleep
Until the resurrection morn.
BENEDICT—Farewell ! my Sister,
We oft shall meet within the Sacred Heart.*
                        [Exit.

* The reader must now bear in mind that SS. Benedict and
Scholastique have been duly consecrated for their offices, and that
the Arch-Monastery and the Convent of the Sacred Heart are in
full working order.

SCENE 7.

Convent Garden—Novices clustering round CLARE *and* ADELE. (*Nuns.*)

JANE (*eldest Novice*)—What said the Abbess when you
  Gave our gifts, and which did she prefer,
  The Gospel of S. John, illuminated since her
  Last birthday by her industrious novices,
  Or the flowers ?
CLARE—She graciously received them both.
JANE—What did she say ?
CLARE—Well, as she took the flowers, she said :
  " Sweet scents, swift vehicles of still sweeter
    thoughts."
ADELE—I like to see flowers growing, but
  They cease to please when gathered, rootless
    things,
  And perishable as frail human life.
JANE—Do you not offer flowers to those you love ?

ADELE—No; nor wish to have them from hands
    dear to me.

JANE—Why! you did bring the white moss rose
    To dear Angela's grave?

ADELE—'Tis true: I took it up a tender plant,
    Just sprouted on a bank exposed,
    Which the next frost had nipp'd;
    And, with a careful hand, transplanted it
    To that blest spot where the sun always
    shines.

JANE—There it has flourished,
    Grown sweet to sense, and lovely to the eye.

ADELE—But as a rule, it is my wish and way
    To let all flowers live freely, and all die
    Among their kindred in their native place.

CLARE—I've noticed often with a pleased surprise
    You never pluck the rose; the violet's head
    Hath shaken with your breath upon its bank
    And not reproached you; the ever sacred cup
    Of the pure lily hath between your hands
    Felt safe, unsoiled, nor lost one grain of gold.

JANE—I wish I had not gathered them.

CLARE—Nay wish not that; the fault be mine
    If any, *she* was pleased ; she said:
    " The flowers were sweet, but not so sweet
    As her dear children's love."
JANE—What said she more ?
CLARE—More! you *are exigeant.*
    Well, then, just I as made my reverence to go,
    She said: " *These* tell the dull, old tale that
        bloom must fade:
This the bright truth that love can never die."
    And as she spoke, she kissed the holy Gospel.
    This is a Festival, so all can now disperse,
    Each to her favourite occupation.
                   [*Exeunt* NOVICES.
ADELE—See! Clare, here Agnes comes,
    Our young Postulant.
[CLARE *goes to meet a young girl who is timidly*
    approaching.
CLARE (*embracing her*)—Agnes, the Abbess bids
    you kindly welcome,
    And therefore you must needs come well to us.
    She will receive, and speak to you to-day.

AGNES—To-day ! long have I wished to see her,
And now I am afraid—what is she like ?
CLARE—She's tall, and gravely sweet
    The impression of her features, which to scan
    Their lofty loveliness forbids : her eyes you'll
        feel, but see not,
    Only on her brow you'll mark a cross described.
    Her voice is peaceful, clear and authoritative ;
    Her manner gentle, tender and serene,
    And inexpressibly sweet,
    Enabling her to say things stern, severe,
    Without offending or repelling hearers.
AGNES—Then, she is beautiful ?
ADELE—Her beauty lacks but halo of the saint,
    Nay, scarcely that.
AGNES—Do you remember what you felt when
    you first saw her ?
ADELE—I do not ; my mind was too confused.
    (*to* CLARE) Do you remember your first
    interview ?
CLARE—O well, 'twas in the Chapel, there she
    stood,

Embalm'd in holy beauty, in her eyes
Downcast and chaste, such sacred influence
    lived,
That none might gaze on their pure spheres,
    and feel
One earth-born longing : serene the light
That floated round her, as the lineaments
It cased with its mild glory.
Lowly I knelt before her, all my senses
    bound
In pleasing awe, and in fond reverence.
AGNES—How does she manage with her faulty
    children ?
CLARE—She ponders well, and understands each
    character :
She never falters, with most she never fails :
Sometimes a compassionate look, sometimes
    a cheerful one
Alights on the earthy thought,
And dries up all its noxiousness.
Like the air that angels breathe
In the great Temple of the Christian World,

Her soul at every season of our tempers
Preserves one temperature.

AGNES—How ! is she always so unchanged ?

CLARE—Unchanged must ever be the blessed
    soul

Who leans in fond security on THE UN-
CHANGED.

AGNES (*after a pause*)—May I now spend
    some time in Chapel,

As we are free from business for the day ?

CLARE (*smiling*)—What a deal of time we lose
    in business !

Go, dearest Agnes, certainly you may.

                    [*Exit* AGNES.

What think you of our new Postulant ?

ADELE—Her devotion is ardent, and her face
    seems prefigured

For the Offices of Adoration.

I like, and I admire her,

Altho' she does not seem of noble birth.

CLARE—You think too much of that—

  But Agnes has no reason to blush at her birth,

The breast which gave her nourishment
    ne'er heaved
With sense of ignominy as she pressed her
    to it.
She loves her mother with affection passionate;
Last night I heard her murmur in her sleep:
" O mother, if such should be GOD's will,
    sometimes
Look down on me when the song to Him is
    suspended;
Oh! look often upon me with prayer and pity."
ADELE—My life for it she will, for there all prayers
Are accepted, and all pity devoid of pain.
Did she awake?
CLARE—No; I gently kissed her, and withdrew:
I could not bear to see those large heavy
    tears following
Heavy and slow, as Nuns at the funeral of a
    Sister.
ADELE—She is my countrywoman, is she not?
CLARE—She is, and loves her native language
    more than the English tongue.

ADELE—Is it a fact the Virgin spoke to her ?

CLARE—It is : about a week ago Agnes,
    In agony of weeping, pray'd before Our
        Lady's shrine :
    Suddenly—these are the girl's own words :
    " Un éblouissement la contraignit de fermer
        les yeux, et elle entendre une voix d'en
        haut, qui lui disait : Pourquoi pleures tu ?
        N'as-tu pas une tendre Mère dans le
        Ciel ? "

ADELE—When did her mother die ?

CLARE—A month ago,
    Leaving to Agnes what she valued most,
    A Rosary strung with beads from Olivet.

ADELE—I've noticed them, they are ever in her
        hands.

CLARE—Daily does Agnes count those beads;
        from each
    The picture of some Christian truth ascending:
    She says the mysteries shine on high to her
    Like Constellations, and our quiet life
    For her to music rolls on poles of love

Thro' realms of Glory; till nothing the present seems,
As one hand touches Calvary, one the Eternal
    Gates.

[*Enter* GRACE, *the youngest orphan, with an empty basket.*

CLARE—(*looks at the empty basket*)—Where are
    its rich contents?
Has Euphemia given them already?

GRACE—I've given them myself, oh, they were
    lovely!
The purple-flowering cactus, and the golden
Lobelia, the woodbine, and the syringa.
You see I've learnt their names,
You could not say them better.

CLARE—Why did you give them?

GRACE—Because Euphemia is a loiterer.

CLARE—Audacious little creature, a loiterer!
    Is that a fit term for Euphemia,
    The mild and bashful girl?

GRACE—Bashful—ah! that is the word I meant
    to say,

Not loiterer. Euphemia said that I might
    give the flowers, because I had come
    later from GOD's Hands.

CLARE—And therefore have got leave to break
    the rule ?

GRACE (*absently*)—What rule ?

CLARE—The orphans' rule, that the youngest
    must take the lowest place,

And obey the Sister who is over them.

Did I not hear the Sister Jane charge Effie to
    give the flowers ?

ADELE—Then Effie broke the rule, not Grace ;
    besides

That rule is sometimes qualified,

I've heard our Abbess say—

CLARE (*interrupts her. Aside.*)—Do not en-
    courage Gracie's petulance,

Say what you mean in French.

Must I remind you . . Ce que recommande
    le plus Saint Benoît a ses Moines, c'est
    l'abnegation et l'obéissance sans réserve
    aux Superieurs.

ADELE (*smiling*)—Mais en prescrivant la sou-
mission a l'Abbé, il veut que celui-ci
n'entreprendrenne rien d'important san
consulter tous ses Frères, en ajoutant que
Dieu révèle souvent un plus jeune ce qui
vaut le mieux : and Effie is our youngest
Novice, altho' the eldest of our orphans.

CLARE—What, Effie be consulted in the
Chapter !

She's not thirteen.

ADELE—Yet still she is a Novice, and surely in
the matter of the flowers had a voice.

Come! Clare forgive the little child; look at her !
How wistfully she gazes at the river !

CLARE (*putting her hand on Grace's shoulder*)—
What are you thinking of ?

GRACE—I'm thinking Effie's like that lily on the
river,

By countless little reeds surrounded (that's
us the younger orphans), at intervals
seen only as they wave about her,
quivering and bending to the breeze.

O, I love, Effie! Yet she gave me pain
to-day.

CLARE—How so?

GRACE—She said she feared the Abbess could
not
Love us all, because there are so many of us.

CLARE—Be not uneasy; and tell dear Effie
The heart of our good Abbess will never dry
up,
So many streams run into it.
How did you give the flowers?

GRACE—I ran after the Abbess as she was
leaving our dormitory, and presented
them on my knees, as the orphans' gift.
She accepted them as kindly as possible,
and bade me be happy.

CLARE—I hope you will always keep her command.

GRACE—No one is unhappy here:
How could they in the Sacred Heart!

CLARE—Bless you dear child! Now run away
To your companions; and don't forget my

Message to Euphemia.

[*She takes the basket from* GRACE *and kisses her.*

GRACE (*running away*)—The heart of our good
      Abbess will never dry up,
So many streams run into it.

ADELE—Sister, the shade of this o'erarching
      canopy
Of trees, suits well with meditation, the sun's
Still warm, we'll rest, and look into the forest.

            [*The Nuns seat themselves.*

CLARE (*taking a withered rose from her bosom*)—
How the heart beautifies the smallest thing!
This withered rose to me 'tis dear, so dear
I would not for the fairest flower exchange.
My Angela brought it to me not long
Before her death, and sadly said—
" I've watered it from the clearest spring,
And yet see how 'tis withering."

ADELE—What did you say?

CLARE—Something to soothe her :
That was the only time I saw her sad.
Joy intense, it was her native element.

D

When the sun rose, her heart leapt with
    delight.
" See, Sister, see ! " she used to say, while
    pointing to the east :
" The Seraph hands · unbar the gates of
    Heaven."
And when I watched her sleep in rosy health,
As peaceable as spotless innocence ;
And radiant (if there yet was light enough
To show it on her face) with pleasant dreams,
Such as young angels come on earth to play
    with ;
Too happy even for hope, maker of happiness,
I would think that for her, surely
Departure from this earth could never be
Departure from its joys : the joys of Heaven
Would mingle with them scarcely with fresher
    sweetness.
ADELE—How is it that she had such difficulty
In learning some of the Commandments?
CLARE—Because she said, " It gave her pain to
    be told

What not to do by one she loved so well as
  GOD."
But when He told her what to do, that gave
  her happiness.
ADELE—Because when He tells us what to do,
  He gives us an opportunity of pleasing Him;
  But when He tells us what not to do, it is a
    sign
  That we have displeased, or are likely to dis-
    please Him.
CLARE—Just so: that was my darling's mean-
    ing.
  O, gracious piece of childhood! would I had
    seen
  Your intelligence developed.
  Would that your days had been lengthened.
ADELE—Have you forgotten the labourers in
    the vineyard?
  Ah! Sister, the years of grown-up people
    will often be
  Counted for nothing. A thousand years are
  But as a night-watch of three hours, and three

Hours of love and adoration may be ten
　　thousand
Times a thousand years.　Does it not make
You glad to know the little stream that lost
Itself so soon in the ocean, ran clear from
　　the first ?
CLARE—It does.　Angela, of this earth ! the
　　brightest flower not cropt,
Transplanted only to immortal bloom
Of love with Saints, and happiness with God !
ADELE—I miss her mostly in the recreation
　　room ;
For there she always brought visionary looks,
And soft, sweet angel-tongue,
And flowers, sweet as herself,
Her baby-hands were impotent to hold.
Her head reminded me of Guido's cherubs ;
How oft have I pressed down her bright
　　curls
With my forefinger, to see them spring up
　　again.
You knew, and loved her mother ?

CLARE—I did ; she died upon my breast
    A few days after Angela was born.
    Her last words were—" Take my babe, when
       'tis weaned
    To Abbess Scholastique." I loved the babe,
    Because it loved me so, that it would leave
    The nurse herself, to come into mine arms.
ADELE—And since her lady-mother, that did die
    In childbed of her, loved you passing well,
    It may be nature fashion'd this affection.
    I was not in the Chapel when Angela died ;
    Her death was very sudden : what think you
    Was the cause of it ?
CLARE—It was her First Communion :
    I noticed when the Priest held up the Host,
    Her bloom all faded, by greater light sub-
      limed :
    " Let me depart ! " she cried, " dear Sister, I
      must go ! "
ADELE—She saw a vision ?
CLARE—A vision the strain'd eyes cannot
    inclose,

Or bring again before them from the senses,
Which clasp it, hang upon it, nor will ever
Release it, following thro' eternity.
ADELE—And with the " Gloria in Excelsis,"
    Her young life passed away ?
CLARE—Yes ; thus she left us, yielding up her
        soul,
    A joyous thank-offering to Him she loved,
    Thus—thus exultingly did she depart,
    Song on her lips, ecstasy in her heart.
                        [*After a pause.*
    I've spoken of my pet to make you better :
                    [*Takes* ADELE's *hand.*
    I cannot bear to see you look so ill.
ADELE—Ah ! Clare, this is the anniversary of
        my shame ;
    Ah me! the thistledown hath weight compared
    With my false promise, and promise made to
        GOD.
CLARE—I've heard how influenced by your
        worldly friends
    You left the life after you were Professed ;

You only stayed away a week, and then
    returned ;
I was not present, but Constance told me all,
How you knelt at the Chapel door,
And how your moans of smothered agony
Conveyed a sense of anguish so intense,
That all the Nuns (who standing, waited for
    the Abbess)
Sunk trembling on their knees, and to your
    groans,
Responded with floods of sobs and tears.
GOD has forgiven you.
ADELE—He *has;* so willingly I can't forgive
    myself.
As soon as I returned, He sent my Angel to me
With flowers not of this earth, the sharp
    thorns round them
Wounded me: "Take them," my Guardian
    said :
" The sharpness of these penitential thorns
Is the first thing felt, but after,
Only the flowers' delicious fragrance.

Keep them in thy heart, they are all dappled
O'er with virtues from the life-blood of the
LAMB that holiness and truth might live in
    you, GOD loved in Him."
I knelt, and placed the flowers upon my
    breast, and said :
" I know not how to thank thee ; rude
I am in speech and manners, but yet there's
    something
In my heart, which makes me bold to say, that
Adele ne'er shall shame this favour : Angel,
These fair flowers by me (if He but please to
    help first gave them)
Shall ne'er be worn upon a heart corrupted.
" I will be sworn they will not," he replied :
And as he spoke, there passed between us
A mutual smile of sympathy and trust,
As though our lots were linked; I knew not
    how.
CLARE—I fain would see these flowers.
ADELE—You shall when I am dead, but not till
    then.

O, Clare ! how gently has our Abbess borne
    with me,
Since first I entered the Religious Life :
Sometimes I fear that I have kept her
    back,
If that were possible.   Do you not think
Small minds are impediments to great ?
Chestnuts and oaks permit the traveller to
    pass on ;
Briars and thorns, and unthrifty grass, en-
    tangle him.
Clare—I grant you've given our good Abbess
    trouble
Which she does not grudge : if she has
    watched you closer,
And made your rule stricter than your
    Sisters, it is
Because large holes in brick walls easily are
    filled up,
But slightest flaw in ruby is irreparable.
Had you remained away from us you would
    have lost these flowers.

What happy impulse moved you to return?
[*The* ABBESS *is approaching them unperceived.*
ADELE—My loved Superior, 'twas thine inspira-
     tion.

She is here! [*The* ABBESS *takes* ADELE *aside.*
ABBESS—You've sent me all the names of your
     sick poor?
ADELE—I have: my work is over now, and it
     has been a failure:

Why did you give me what I could not do?
ABBESS—That it was difficult, I know full well.
There are few works of piety which require
     such patience, such tenderness, such
     self-mortification, and frequently such
     skilful tact, as the visitation of abodes
     where misery, pain, disappointment,
     ignorance, and often vice, meeting to-
     gether, form one great social, corporal,
     and spiritual wound. Still were you
     not fitted for the work, I should not
     have assigned it unto you.
                    [*Looking at* ADELE *kindly.*
My child, you suffer!

Great drops of sweat they stand upon your brow,
Like a cold winter dew.

ADELE—Mother forgive, if for a moment, pain-
tossed,
I forgot respects that are religious.
I have not done my duty to the poor :
Ah! there are little things that leave no
little regrets ;
I might have said kind words, and have done
kind actions to many who are now
beyond the reach of them.

ABBESS—Kind thoughts unspoken may reach
them yet.

ADELE—It is a sweet thought, and comforting ;
And I am grateful—I have been strangely blest.
Why has GOD given me so much ?

ABBESS—*Because He loves you :* we think too
much upon *what* GOD has given us, and
too little *why.* (*After a pause*)—My child,
I've read the note you sent to me last
night ; your thoughts run deep, and you
do well to speak of them to me alone ; the
Sisters might perhaps misunderstand you.

ADELE—Thank God   for by your gentle words
You show you are not angry with my note.

ABBESS—Angry ! did not our blessed LORD
Himself express a wish in His last hours
on earth, that the bitter cup might pass
away from Him; and if you in humble
imitation, dared to implore that a more
bitter cup might be removed from the
vast body of mankind ; a cup containing
the poison of eternal punishment, where
agony succeeds to agony, but never death
—O GOD ! shall I blame you ? No ! by
CHRIST's sufferings, no ! (*Looks anxiously
at* ADELE.) Your worn looks grieve me,
but for that I would not part with you
just yet, I have so much to say, so much
to hear from you ; I hear you pacing up
and down at night; what makes you do so?

ADELE—Mother, I cannot sleep for thinking of
The Inner Life, the Mystery of Being,
Heaven, Hades, Hell, the Eternal How and
Where,

The glory of the dead, and their despair :
And O Eternity! the ALMIGHTY's Life Time,
When millions of ages, a million times told
    over,
Have rolled away, even then that Eternity .
Stands forth unimpaired, undiminished.
ABBESS—Daughter, your thoughts are wearing
    out your frame;
No human mind can grasp these things.
ADELE—Mine made the attempt, only to fall
    back
Upon itself, weak, helpless, and confused.
ABBESS—Then think of JESUS only.
                 [*Takes her hand.*
Heaven! what a wasted little hand.
And your poor eyes are sunk, and dark with
    tears.
ADELE—Yet I am happy, for I hear His voice
Who bade men weep that so they might
    rejoice.
ABBESS—His peace be with you.
I'll not detain you longer from repose,

Which you so sadly want;
Again, GOD bless thee !
ADELE—Good-night, my Mother :
Health has forsaken me ;
I feel 'twill not be long 'ere thou shalt see
Another cross in our dear Cemetery,
O then look on it, and remember
My spirit will be soothed to hear once more
" GOD bless thee ! " kindly spoken as you
    did just now.
And if in past sweet converse I have had
    with you,
My too bold spirit, and your condescension
    led me
Beyond the awful limits to be observed
By one so much beneath your sacred person,
I thus low crave your gracious pardon.
                                    [Kneels.
ABBESS—(*raising and embracing her*) 'Tis hard
    to lose you even for a time :
You'll pray for me when you are there,
There, where one loving word

Alone is never heard,
That loving word—*farewell.*
ADELE—It almost sends me forward on my way,
To receive and welcome you ;
Few are the Spirits of the Glorified
I'd spring to earlier at the Gate of Heaven.
[*She embraces the* ABBESS, *and they both walk
slowly towards the Convent,* ADELE
leaning on the arm of the ABBESS.

SCENE 8.

*A splendid Autumn evening.—Convent of the
Sacred Heart.—The* ABBESS *in her Cell.
—A gentle knock at the door.*

ABBESS—Peace be unto you ! *
[*Enter* PORTRESS. *She makes a reverence.*
PORTRESS—A young girl wants to see you.
ABBESS—Who is she ?

* Without this salutation no one could enter the presence of the
Abbess.

PORTRESS—I cannot tell, for she is veiled.

ABBESS—How do you know then that she's
    young ?

PORTRESS—By her slight form, and timid speech.

ABBESS—Bid her come up.

PORTRESS—She's here.

[*Exit* PORTRESS. *Enter a girl who drops her veil
    and falls on her knees.*

ABBESS (*aside*)—Had one the choice of all earth's
    loveliest figures,

  One could not take form of more glorious
    sweetness.

(*Aloud*)—What do you wish, my child ?

GIRL—I wish to be Professed at once.

ABBESS—Does this wish rise because that none
  Hath won that little heart of thine at present ?

GIRL—Many have won it, Mother-Lady,

  I never see one run across the road

  To help a lame man, or guide the blind,

  But that one wins it ; I never hear one speak

  As all should speak of you, but, up my arms

  Fly ready to embrace him !

ABBESS—And when any
  Says thou art beautiful, and says he loves
    thee,
  What is your heart then ready for ?
GIRL—To me none ever said such things ; I see
  You do not know me since my glorious vision:
  Mother, I am your godchild, Lucy.
ABBESS—Lucy ! you remind me strongly of
    her—but—
GIRL—Lucy transfigured you would say :
  Hear me, my Mother, reverend and dear,
  'Tis but a few hours since,
  GOD's Mother deigned to appear to me,
  And gave me the vocation of a Nun.
  With those clear rays which she infused on me,
  That beauty am I blessed with, which you
    see.
ABBESS—Thou dost not need probation after
    such a call.
  Rise Lucy, look, how grand !
[*Points to the stars, and moon rising over the distant hills.*

E

ABBESS—How wonderful these constellations,
  By the Omnipotent fiat flashed forth
From awful non-existence.
And yet one single soul's more wondrous
    than all worlds
Which map the skies with miracles of
    light.
LUCY (*looking up*)—Mother, what Temple such a
    roof can boast !
What flickering lamp with the rich starlight
    vies!
See, the round moon rests like the Sacred
    Host,
Upon the azure altar of the skies.
ABBESS (*smiling*)—Mary has made you eloquent,
    as well as beautiful.
LUCY—The air is warm; what makes it so
    delicious ?
ABBESS—'Tis balmy with the rich odours of the
    cedar and the acacia.
LUCY—The moon still rises; 'twill be a gorgeous
    night.

ABBESS (*absently*)—Just such a night as one
would like to pass
In converse sweet with Benedict,
Mingling past memories with shadowy
dreams,
And straying along from bygones to futurity.
                    [*Looking at* LUCY
You must go now, my child,
Good-night; I long to see thee as a
Cloistered Nun, kneeling before the Altar.
LUCY—When will that be?
ABBESS—On All Saints Day, if thou canst
wait till then.
LUCY—A month, a long, long month.
ABBESS—Which thou must spend in prayer and
meditation.
LUCY—And then I'll take the vows, and see
Your Church ablaze with lovely flowers.
ABBESS—And then, my child, shalt thou,
The loveliest flower, by JESUS CHRIST be
gathered.
Till then, farewell!

Lucy—Jesu preserve your saintly reverence !

[*She kisses the hand of the* Abbess, *and exit.*
(*The moon rises higher; the calm becomes intense,*
till not a leaf stirs.)

Abbess—I almost think I hear faint fragments
of the songs above.

[*She sits in deep thought till she is roused by the*
sound of sobbing which comes from the
next cell occupied by the youngest Novice *;*
the Abbess *rises, and, going quickly into*
the cell, finds Effie *sitting up in bed weep-*
ing. The Abbess *sits by her.*

Abbess—What ails my sweet Scotch lassie ?
I hear your heart in full, thick beat.

Effie—Mother, this silence is to me appalling ;
But a more awful silence will prevail
On that great day, after the graves have
given up
Their countless dead, and the cry for mercy
dies away.
O ! then, in that moment, fearful of suspense,
The air will be motionless as it is just now :

Not a leaf to stir, and not a wing to cleave
  it.
And then, and then . . . *(in great agita-*
  tion)
Oh, mother! if I should not after all be
  saved.
ABBESS—My poor, poor child.
You have brought here the evil, and the
  good,
Of your grand, gloomy Northern home.
There is too much of terror in your faith.
          [*Signs her with the Cross.*
EFFIE—There is; but as you made that holy
  sign,
I felt more trustful and courageous.
ABBESS—Repeat the "Credo" till you fall
  asleep,
As a child in distress hides its face in its
  mother's lap,
So Effie we may hide ourselves from dreadful
Possibilities, under the shadow of GOD's
  Love.

EFFIE—Thanks, dearest mother; forgive me
for disturbing you. I shall do so no more.
[*She lies down.   Exit* ABBESS.

SCENE 9.

Convent of the Sacred Heart.—ADELE's *Cell.*
ADELE *very ill in bed.   The* ABBESS *sits by*
her.

ADELE—It must have been a lovely sight.
Tell me about it, Mother?
ABBESS—It is impossible to tell you all,
But what I can, I will.
The Ceremony took place at the great
Minster.
We had a High Mass, of course.
Fired by the love that mocks at rest,
Lucy had passed the night before in prayer.

When the day dawned she slept; five hours she
Slept; the sixth she woke,
Rising from happy sleep, and Heaven-sent
    dreams,
Went forth upon her youthful front that
    light,
Which shines from spotless soul.
Then we all went with her to the Minster.
Scarce had she touched within the Chancel
    gates, when lo !
A murmuring music sprang, as if its own,
It welcomed to its bosom, with soft joy
Rejoicing inwardly. The sacred ground to
    this pre-mortal music vibrating thro' the
    aisles ;
The finite mingling with the Infinite.
I looked, but could not see the Altar ; it was
Veiled in clouds of coloured incense.
Softest tints of purpled snow,
Clouds of fire, and rose-hues blended,
Green, and red, and gold ascended.

ADELE—Did Lucy kneel near you ?
ABBESS—Yes ; Lucy was at my side,
 At that tremendous moment, when by words
 Chanted in whispers, from His high abode
 The SON of GOD mysteriously drawn down,
 Enters the consecrated elements. . . .
 When Mass was ended, Lucy was Professed,
 In divine quiet hushed, and wonder-awed,
 She knelt before the Altar, o'er her head
 That veil was flung which woman parts from
  man,
 To make her more than woman.
 And when she took the vows
 Her dark eyes flashed, a visible flash
 Of that invisible lightning, which from GOD
 Vibrates ethereal through the world of souls.
ADELE—Where is she now ?
ABBESS—I left her in the Minster,
 Where she still kneels, and from the altar
 Of a pure heart sends to GOD, thoughts like
 Herself, white, innocent, vows purer, and of
  a sweeter flame than all earth's odours.

ADELE—Dear Lucy, the temper of an angel
    reigns in thee !
  Nature pick'd several flowers from her choice
    banks,
  And bound them up in thee, sending thee
    forth
  A posy for the bosom of the KING of KINGS.
  Mother, do let me see her now ?
ABBESS—No, not to-night, you are too much
    exhausted; so is she.
  Good-night, and may the dew of sleep fall
    gently on you !
[ADELE *falls asleep while the* ABBESS *is blessing*
    her.
ABBESS—(*looking at her*) Farewell my child, thou
    faithfullest and meekest,
  It lies in sight the blessed Rest thou seekest,
  And gently wilt thou pass to it, for thou
  Art all but disembodied even now !
                                    [*Exit.*

SCENE 10.

*Convent of the Sacred Heart.—The Convent
School Children assembling.—Enter* CLARE
and CONSTANCE.

———

CLARE—Sister, will you take all the school to-
    day ?
For I have been with Adele thro' the night.
CONSTANCE—How is she?   Methought I heard
    last night
More than one footstep in her cell.
CLARE—The priest and doctor both were there.
CONSTANCE—Then she is worse ?
CLARE (*whispers*)—Peace to her gentle spirit.
CONSTANCE—She is departed !
CLARE—Hush !   I do not wish the children to
    know yet.
CONSTANCE—'Twill be a sad grief to our
    Abbess.
How does she seem to bear it ?

CLARE—As yet she does not know; I had no
heart to rouse her from her rest.

Come aside a little while.

CONSTANCE—We may not leave the children by
themselves;

Speak in my native language, they'll not
understand.

CLARE—Sa vie s'exhala au premier coup de
l'Ave Maria ; dans un soupir si faible,
qu'il fut à peine entendu'des personnes
qui entouraient son lit.

CONSTANCE—Ce n'est pas une mort, c'est le
doux passage d'une âme pure dans le
sein de Dieu.

       [*She covers her face.*

CLARE—Weep not ! I have shed all your tears
. . . . not all . . . . they burst from me
again.

[*Turns away from the children and weeps bitterly.*

CONSTANCE (*goes after her*)—Dear Sister, I have
not wept at all ;

At least but very little ; but you distress me—

And yet these bitter tears give ease,
And some angry demon knows it, and presses
My temples that there shall fall but few.

[*Enter the* ABBESS.

ABBESS (*to* CONSTANCE)—Go to the School; it
waits for you.

[CONSTANCE *makes a reverence and exit.*

CLARE (*to herself*)—My angel, help me how to
break the melancholy news!

ABBESS—You must to bed, you've been with
Adele longer than you ought.

CLARE—Mother I could not leave her, for she
looked paler, and spoke more feebly than
usual.

And as I helped her into bed, she murmured:
" Faintness hath so usurped upon my knees,
That kneel I cannot; worn with the body's
weight,
My prostrate soul lies, thrown down at thy
feet,
My sweetest SAVIOUR."

ABBESS—Did she sleep well ?

CLARE—Not till the morning dawned, and then
Slumber came over her, some faint sobs broke
it ;
She pressed my hand, and her smile sank
away—
And then came heavier slumber ; nought broke
that.

ABBESS—Thanks be to GOD !
He giveth His beloved sleep.

CLARE (*agitated*)—Mother ! suppose it's death ?

ABBESS (*calmly*)—My child, I do.
'Tis of all sleeps the sweetest.   [*she weeps.*

CLARE (*weeping*) — Dear Margaret laid her
out ;
. And she looks beautiful—
A cross of lilies on her breast,
A crown of roses on her head.
     [*Enter* MARGARET *and* EFFIE *both weeping.*

ABBESS (*looking up*)—Whence comes this wondrous fragrance ?

EFFIE (*timidly*)—I have just emptied my apron
full of lilies. upon the Virgin's Shrine,
and partly from the lilies, and partly
from the blessed angels who were present,
the oratory was filled with fragrance.

ABBESS—Dear child 'tis not of that I speak.
Margaret, whence comes this fragrance ?

MARGARET—It comes from flowers I found on
Adele's breast.

ABBESS—What flowers ?

MARGARET—Mother, I never saw so exquisite !
They rest upon her heart ; the lilies of a purity
whiter than snow, the roses of Divine
Love, the blue cyanias of Heavenly meditation, and the dark violets of nightly
prayer.

EFFIE—Shall we adorn her grave with them ?

ABBESS—Adorn a grave !
And lose their freshness amongst bones and
rottenness !
And have their odour stifled in the dust !
Nay, put them on the Altar, not on any grave

Save His which never saw corruption.
I love sweet odours; surely my LORD Himself
Must have breathed His very spirit into these!
Let me smell them again; let me inhale them
Into the sanctuary of my heart, lighted up
By His love for their reception.
CLARE (*still weeping*)—O potent flowers! woven
      for thee Adele,*
By Heaven's Messenger; virtues which thou
      hast
Never scattered, never lost, whose native air
      is Heaven.
ABBESS (*wipes her eyes*)—Come! she rests well,
      and we do ill to idle thus—
Let's to our daily work; you (*to* CLARE) to
      bed:
And Margaret, haste thee to the western wing,
And learn if the aged Pilgrim dozes yet;
Effie, you attend the little orphan boys,
And when their task is done, prepare their
      breakfast;

* See p. 40.

But scant the allowance of the red hair'd
  urchin,
That maim'd the poor man's cur.

[Exeunt.

SCENE 11.

A luxuriously furnished room in an old Castle,
within view of the Sacred Heart.—LADY
AUGUSTA; *her maid* DORA *sits listlessly at*
her feet embroidering.

LADY A.—Sing to me something pretty.
DORA (*sings*)—" Life comes without consent;.
  Life leaves us just the same,
None knowing why it went,
None knowing why it came:
  I live because I must,
  I never willed it so,
And I shall turn to dust
  Whether I like, or no."

LADY A.—You do not surely think that pretty?
    Where did you get it?
DORA—The music's from an ancient ballad,
The words are all my own.
LADY A.—In them you do very little remember
Either womanhood, or Christianity:
'Twould make your good mother sigh
To hear you sing such stuff.
       [DORA *turns aside and covers her face.*
LADY A.—What disturbs you?
DORA—O! a crowd of old thoughts your words
    have stirred. Mother! dear, faithful,
    tender soul—I feel the loving tremble of
    your hand upon my own, as solemnly
    this moment as if it had been the rustle
    of an Angel's wing!
LADY A. (*puts down her work*)—Forgive me,
    I'm sorry I have spoken of her, and she
    so lately gone.
DORA—It does me good: O, for that time! . .
    When—but one moment of it—
    My hand in her's, or her's upon my head.

My mother! O my mother! while I repeat
That name again, freshness breathes over me.
What is there like it? Why, 'tis like sweet
    hay
To rest upon after a twelve hours' march ;
Clover, with all its flowers, an arm's length
    deep.
Every thought of her
Engenders a warm sigh within me, which,
Like curls of holy incense, overtake
Each other in my bosom, and enlarge
With their embrace her sweet remembrance.
LADY A. (*aside*)—Strange! what eloquence
        about what seemed to me a very
        commonplace old woman.
(*Aloud*)—Dora you are gifted, and would have
        been a wondrous woman were you of
        good birth and education.
DORA—I would be anything, but what I am.
    Not that I want to be of higher birth,
    Or better education; but, oh! I long for
    A holier life, and one devoted to

God's service and the suffering Poor.
Lady, I have been with you now ten years ;
Let's not grow old together as many
Ladies, and their women do,
With talking nothing, and with doing less :
Let's not spend all our life in that which
Least concerns life, only in sleeping,
Eating, putting on our clothes.
[LADY A. *suddenly rises and goes to the window.*]
LADY A.—Dora, let's go into the Sacred Heart.
DORA—That was my wish—but—
LADY A.—I'll have no buts, and no delay—
For lunacy, or else the devil himself
Will take possession of me.
DORA—Ah, Lady, I've no dowry.
LADY A.—The Sacred Heart does not enforce a
dowry.
But now I think on't, I have not been a
generous mistress to thee—I have given
good words, but no deeds : Now's the
time to requite all :
I will pay down your dowry.

Come, go with me at once ;
And let the last act be the best i' the play,
And then rest, gentle bones.

[*Exeunt.*

SCENE 12.

Recreation Room in the Sacred Heart.—CON-
STANCE *and* AUGUSTA *embroidering an
Altar-cloth.*

CONSTANCE—There so strange a unity of thought
  Between us, that before I knew it so,
  I should have thought it quite impossible.
AUGUSTA—To one great Hand I do attribute
      this,
  And think He has engraven these same lines
  In your soul, as on mine.
CONSTANCE—Two instruments, I've heard it
      stated,
  When strung and tuned in unison ;

The dulcet notes evoked by one,
By echo, are communicated to the other,
And equal concord doth appear.
But tell me truly, was it *ennui* brought you
    here ?
AUGUSTA—That, and that only, I assure you ;
And therefore am I kept so long a Novice.
CONSTANCE—And Dora was Professed at once.
AUGUSTA—Ah ! yes, my darling Dora came from
    higher cause ;
For praise to God, and good to man she came.
CONSTANCE—Her's was a blessed death I've
    heard.
AUGUSTA—And bright and beautiful !
The day before she died she said to me :
" A calm comes over me, life brings it not
With any of its tides : my end is near :
When I am gone think of me, but not often,
For fear my faults should burthen your
    affection."
CONSTANCE—Was not the Abbess with her when
    . she passed away ?

AUGUSTA—She was, Dora (who did not know her
    till she spoke)
  Said "Where is the Abbess?
  Let me but take her blessing up to Heaven,
  And I shall go with confidence."
  "Dora, my child!" the Abbess said:
  "May that pure bliss just Heaven
  Bestows upon departed Saints be thine!"
  Then Dora looking up, exclaimed: "I come!
    I come!
  Ye Sons of Light now take me on your
    wings."
  Then from her lips pealed forth that great
    triumphant
  Chant sung by the Virgin Mother.
               And so she passed away.
CONSTANCE—O blissful transit!
  The earth lie light upon her, and the flowers
  That grow about her, flourish and sweetly
    smell.
                 [After a pause.
  You wish to know what brought me here?

AUGUSTA—You know I do.

CONSTANCE—Well then: at sixteen years I fell
  in love; the love was not returned;
And I grew desperate.

AUGUSTA—Then misery brought you—
  Ah! man may scoff, the Sacred Heart will
  reject none.

CONSTANCE—I did not even know of such a place
Till I was taken to it: It happened thus:
One evening I walked forth, not knowing,
And not caring where I went: tired out at last
I threw myself upon the ground, and wept:
And as I wept, upon my shoulder sank a hand,
I turned, it was a noble lady clothed in black,
And veil'd: that veil thrown back, I recog-
  nised
At once the luminous stillness which the
  Cloister breeds.
A voice as pure and calm as if from Heaven,
Addressed me thus: "Why do you weep?
The Sacred Heart is near." My hand lurk'd
  soon

In her's, compulsion soft drew me magnetic to
This very room, where sat three Nuns,
    Margaret,
Adèle and Clare; the latter read aloud how
    Saints
Have suffered, and how glorious their reward.
Then sang these childless ones of Bethlehem's
    Child.
And then I followed them into the Chapel,
There my limbs failed me, and I swooned.
I'm told I lay as dead, until the Abbess shook
Dews from the Font above me! and I awoke
With heart emancipate that outsoared the lark.
It was as though some child that dreaming,
    wept
Its childish plaything lost, by bell awaked,
Bride-bells, had found herself a queen,
    New wed unto her Country's Lord.
AUGUSTA—What! were you then Professed at
    once?
CONSTANCE—Almost! because the Abbess said:
" That my vocation was so strongly marked."

And here I've lived a rapturous life
Of Christian freedom, mask'd in what but
Servitude had been to one lacking vocation
    true.
            [*As she speaks* CLARE *enters.*
Life hid with GOD ! 'tis hidden from the world,
Lest virtue should be dimm'd by virtue's
    praise.
CLARE—Here noble natures cast out bitterness,
  And o'er the scar, like pine tree uncorrupt,
  Weep healing gums; till all the Inner
    Being
  Freed from asperities, in the Light of GOD
  Shines, like the feet of my blest Crucifix
    Kissed into smoothness.
  Here sweets are sweeter for the rain,
  And growth stronger for shadow.
CONSTANCE—Here blest contrition has its place
  Beside untarnished innocence; the Magda-
    lene ascetic,
  And the Virgin pure, the Sacred Heart gladly
    receiveth both !

AUGUSTA—Sisters, I am not worthy of my lot :
  I think I ought to put off my Profession;
          To-morrow is too soon.
CLARE—Ah, that reminds me to tell you, Con-
      stance,
  That you must have more incense for to-
      morrow.
  The incense lately has too feebly floated,
                        [*Smiling.*
  Like holy thoughts sent feebly up
  From soul of feeble Saint.
                    [*Turning to* AUGUSTA.
  And you, oh! do not fear—
  You may be sure that from the Vow
  Which binds the will's infinitude to GOD, up-
      wells,
  That peaceful strength, whose fount is GOD.
  From Him, behind His sacramental veil,
  In holy passion, for long hours adored,
  Comes that great love which makes the bonds
      of earth
          Needless, thence irksome.

AUGUSTA—As the gracious tree draws the poor
  creeper
On the ground diffused, and lifts it into light,
So have your words to me.
And now I must retire myself a little to
  prepare
    To meet the blessing of to-morrow.
[AUGUSTA *exit : she enters the Chapel, and, fall-
  ing prostrate before the Statue of Mary,
  she murmurs.*
Mother, forgive these tears.
Showers sometimes fall upon a shining day,
. I ne'er was truly happy till this hour.
To-morrow, oh ! to-morrow—
My joy chokes up my words.
                    [*The Angelus sounds.*

PART SECOND.

Scene 13.

Garden of the Arch-Monastery—Maur,* Bernard,† *and* Sylvester *walking in it.*—
Placidus *meets them, and kneels before Maur.*

Placidus—Are you at leisure, reverend Father,
    now ?
Maur—Why, Son, you made confession yester-
    day.
Placidus—Let me again, for I would empty
    This vessel of myself of all the dregs, (which
    since
    My last confession cleared me) have

---

* Maur, Assistant-Superior Priest and Monk.
 † Bernard is the Abbot's Guardian Angel under the habit of a
young Monk.

Taken again a habitation in me;
And with a powerful sweet acknowledg-
    ment,
Hunt out those spirits which haunt this
    house of flesh.
MAUR—Thou'rt right, and it is well to weep for
    sins;
(Tears make dry branches flourish green and
    fresh)
And to confess them frequently, if you
Thereby are helped on in the narrow path.
PLACIDUS—The oft'ner that I cast my reckoning
    up,
I find my sleep the sounder.
MAUR—I'll be well pleased to hear thee,
    And did I not, the Saints of Heaven
Would knit their brows at me.
                    [*Exeunt* MAUR *and* PLACIDUS.
SYLVESTER—Bernard, how is it that you don't
    go to Confession ? *
BERNARD—I have gone to the Abbot.

* The first Benedictines knew nothing of Compulsory Confession.

SYLVESTER—But very seldom ; you have peculiar
     notions on the subject, which I should
     like to know ;
I fancy they are somewhat like my own.
BERNARD—My thoughts are at your service—
I think .   .   .
SYLVESTER—I'm all attention ; haste, for it is
     close upon the Angelus.
BERNARD (*speaking rapidly*) — Conscience of
     man ! how awful is its power,
The system of Auricular Confession testifies,
And to that burden terrible of solitude :
But still it seems to me a poor resource
To make a Confessor out of an accomplice ;
For the heart into which we pour our con-
     fession,
Has its own memories of guilt and pain,
. And these, my brother, make it hard at times,
And therefore misjudging to the sinner,
Even when it is tolerant to sin.
Struggles there are, and sins that must be
     dumb,

And only come to GOD with tears and groans :
CHRIST will not despise the misery of those
Who cannot speak, and make appeal to Him
Alone, who knows them better than they know
Themselves, and has chief power to help them.
SYLVESTER—Ay, Bernard, thou'rt right :
    Auricular Confession, it is often good,
    If not compulsory ; but not for every soul :
    It is not indispensable, nor all prevailing in
        its help ;
    Because no saint on earth can read the heart.
BERNARD—Sylvester, it is well that from each
        other
    God has hid our hearts ;
    And left them open only to Himself,
    And beings of a better world, who can
    Look in upon us with more loving eyes,
    Because they have a larger share
    In the Divine intelligence.
[*The Angelus sounds, and the Monks fall on
        their knees.*

SCENE 14.

*The Guests' Room in the Arch-Monastery.—
Fitzroi reading by the light of a flickering
lamp—The clock strikes twelve.*

FITZROI (*reads*)—" Ferte fortiter : hoc est quo
　　　Deum antecedatis.

Ille enim extra patientiam malorum, vos-
　　　supra.

Contemnite dolorem ; aut solvetur, aut solvet.

Contemnite fortunas, nullus telum, quo
　　　feriret amimum habet."*

FITZROI—I used to say these words to broken
　　　hearts ;

And gave them what I thought was good
　　　advice.

O the good GOD of GODS,

---

* Bear yourself with fortitude; by this means you surpass the
Gods ; for they are out of the reach of misfortunes, you superior
to them. Despise pain : it will either be destroyed, or it will destroy
you. Be indifferent to circumstances. No one has a weapon to
strike the mind.

How blind is pride! what eagles we are still
  In matters that belong to other men !
  What beetles in our own !
Would I were dead : (oh, plague !)
Hence, mocking wretch.
                [*Throws the book aside.*
Thou wrapt in furs, basking thy limbs 'fore
  fires,
Forbid'st the frozen zone to shudder.
Thou foamy bubbling of a Stoic's brain—
          [*He rises and paces the room.*
O Eva, may my depth of love for thee
Damn all my comforts to a lasting fast
From every joy of life !
         [*He groans. Enter the* ABBOT.
ABBOT—What dost thou up at midnight ?
[*Takes up the book which Fitzroi has thrown
  down.*
You've left your Psalter for this heathen lore;
Wert thou a Brother, not a guest,
Thou should'st have penance most severe for
  this.

FITZROI—Oh, my Lord Abbot, leave me!
  You see how less than man I am.
ABBOT—I dare not leave you longer thus alone.
                    Take comfort.
FITZROI—Confusion to all comfort!   I defy it.
ABBOT—Pray you be more patient.
FITZROI—Pigmy woes can shelter under
      patience's shield;
  But giant grief will burst all covert. .
ABBOT—Forbear these starts of passion,
  Or I will leave you wedded to despair,
  As you are now.   Have you forgot your GOD?
  What is now 'twixt you and Him?
  A will uncrucified, a soul's revolt.
  O dreadful answer!   I am ashamed . to see
      you.
  Yet you move me; and even tho' my words
  Accuse me justly, I almost weep with you,
  When you go to your Eva's grave and kneel,
  And press your brow against the Cross,
  With moans that make the marble sweat with
      pity.

. . . We must all die, all leave ourselves.

It matters not when, where, or how, so we
    die well.

And can Evangeline need lamentation for
    her ?

Her last words were : (must I remind you of
    them) ?

" Give all yourself to GOD ; and as you love
    me,

Do not over love me."   I charge you by the
    love you owe her,

And as you hope for blessing from her
    prayers,

To be more worthy of what her last will, not
    your

Merit gave you ! her undying love.

                 [FITZROI *groans.*

No memory of her so holy life, but should
    have power

To frustrate all the juggling deceits,

By which the devil binds you to a selfish
    sorrow.

Have you no duty to your precious child?

FITZROI—I have, I have.   O, how she loved that
    boy!

She thought the day too short to gaze upon
    him,

That all the blessings she could gather for
    him

Were little for her fondness to bestow.

O Heaven, she was all Thine, all Heavenly.

      [*He turns to the* ABBOT.

I'll not expostulate again

With GOD's decrees.   There is divinity about
    you

That rebukes my selfish, swollen passion.

Good Father, speak once more, and I will

Kneel and listen here as reverently

As to an angel.   If I breathe too loud

. Tell me, for I would be as still as night.

       [*Kneels.*

ABBOT (*laying his hands on* FITZROI's *head*)—

  O JESUS, let no selfish spot dwell in him!

And all his blood's affections, but Thy love

Let him bequeath to earth! O hear me
    Heaven!
Give him a spirit, noble and angelic,
Fit for yourselves to give, and him to offer!
And may his longings after Nature's plea-
    sures,
Feeling but once the fires of nobler thoughts,
Fly, like the shapes of clouds we form, to
    nothing.
Rise now, and rest in peace.
FITZROI (*rising*)—You've ta'en a mass of lead
    from off my heart.
           I'm very weary, Father.
ABBOT—I'faith thou look'st sunk-eyed; go rest
    thy head;
These three days have your eyelids kept
    asunder,
'Tis time that they should meet.
And make good use of your short visit
    here.
FITZROI—I'll pass the remainder in close re-
    treat.

ABBOT—Yes, and before the Cross;
  Till at its foot the passion-flower of self-
    sacrifice
  Takes root, and flourishes.

[*Exit* ABBOT.

SCENE 15.

The ABBOT *sits in the Monastery Garden, looking at some rare plants that lie uprooted
before him.—Enter* FITZROI; *The* ABBOT *rises
and greets him.*

ABBOT—My son, I see delighted, in thy face,
  What was not there before, unearthly calm.
FITZROI—Father, as I knelt just now
  Before the Virgin and the Holy Child,
  Something enforced me to kiss the Child:
  O GOD, the marvellously tranquillising
  Effect of the contact of my lips with those of

Mary's Child! Moses died of the kisses of
GOD's lips. Died! Yes, I know what that
    tradition means.
ABBOT—You still love Evangeline?
FITZROI—I must not say *more* than ever; *better*
    than ever.
ABBOT—It grieves us you must go.
FITZROI—I may return some day.
ABBOT—GOD grant it!
FITZROI—Before I leave you, Father, will you
    From my full heart take what lies deepest
        there,
    And what GOD wills as well as sacrifice.
    My love, my deep thanksgivings; thee I hail,
    Father of the Monastic Life! Can words,
    Can deeds requite the debt we owe to thee?
    You will not hear the voices that all speak
    Your merits, and I thank GOD
    That fame obsequious to base heads
    For once is loyal, and its crown hath laid
    Where honour's debt is due.
    But though you hear no praises,

There are who sing them to their harps on
    high,
And He who can alone reward you,
Listens in all His brightness to the song.
ABBOT (*gravely*)—Low must be those whom
    mortals can sink lower,
Nor high are they whom human power may
    raise ;
But He alone, who made me what I am,
Can make me greater, or can make me less.
GOD grant I work my work : that which I
    am,
He knows who made me : pray for me,
That I fall not at the end. Farewell ; and
Take these flowers (*gives him the plants*) and
    while
They still are fresh, plant them on Eva's
    grave :
Perhaps they'll win some sanctity
By shedding bloom above so pure a breast.
[FITZBOI *takes the plants, makes a reverence, and*
    exit.

Scene 16.

The Arch-Monastery.—The ABBOT *sits, and* FITZROI *stands by his side at an open window which looks into the Garden.*

———

ABBOT—So you, and George both wish to cast
    your lots with ours ?

FITZROI—We do. Is it not better to be such
    as these (*points to some Monks working in
    the Garden*), than be the thing I am ?

ABBOT—What makes you think so ?

FITZROI—I've thought so long before I could
    Make up my mind to come to you.

ABBOT—Since when ?

FITZROI—Since I first saw you sleeping in the
    garden.

ABBOT—How ! saw me sleeping ?

FITZROI—Some years ago, when George was
    little,

I passed with him before the Cloister gates :

They were wide open, so we both went in.
Methought the Cloister's deep repose calmed
    down
The thirst of idle fame, and made me muse
With wiser feelings; for I paused, and looked,
With a pleased sadness, and gazed around,
And sighed, and said it was a blessed
    place;
And I *was* blessed, for I encountered Maur:
And while we talked, George ran into the
    garden;
I followed, and I found him gazing at thee,
My lord, thou slept beneath that grand old
    tree;
                 [Points to a large oak.
And then he scattered flowers all over thee;
The Monks forbade him, saying: " Lest thou
    wake
The Abbot."   But you awoke, and saw the
    boy, and said:
" Forbid him not."
ABBOT—Now I remember, and I said to him:

" Wilt thou stay here ? " and he replied : " I
    will."
He was a most angelic child.
FITZBOI—And has fulfilled the promise of his
    childhood :
In listening to his talk, I hear philosophy of
    Heaven.
I had some happy hours with him last night ;
I staid with him till sunrise : he watched
It wistfully, and said : " The day breaks
    glorious, but oh !
There is a Sun, ten thousand times more
    glorious
Than that which rises in the east, attracts
    me
To rise from earth, and no more to turn
    back,
But for a burial. Why should we care for
    anything
But GOD ? or look upon the world but to
    contemn it ?"
My George's spirit purged, and purified,

Shakes off the clogs of sensuous frailty;
But mine, a dunghill mind composed of
    earth,
In that gross element had happiness
Till Eva died, then chaos of distraction fell
    on me.
ABBOT—'Tis strange and sad so many souls
Cannot look steadfastly at the next world,
Until the light of this one is extinguished.
Your wish to leave the world all understand.
. But George, who with all his piety is naturally
    gay,
For him to leave all pleasures that the earth
    can yield,
That nature can bestow, or art invent,
To undergo the penance of a Cloister—
Does he not value his advantages ?
FITZROI—No ; though descended in a line
    direct
From the old Roman heroes, having by birth
These titles : " Duke of the Golden Fleece;"
" Knight of the Royal Garter; "

" First Lord of the Campagna ; "
And—
ABBOT (*interrupting him and smiling*)—Titles of
    honour add not to his worth,
Who is himself an honour to his titles.
I know the youth : he would, like Maur,
Be Priest as well as Monk.
FITZROI—And has expressed this wish
    In words of touching beauty.
ABBOT—He has : his " Songs of Love Divine "
    (Those love-songs best and sweetest !)
    His " Sacred Warfare of the Realm of
        Souls;"
    "The Anguish;" and "The Cleansing;"
        and "The Crown,"
    Find ever echo in my children's breasts :
    They've even found a way into the " Sacred
        Heart."
    Your noble child covets a nobler name
    Than all his ancestors :
    Such commands he longs to give
    As angels execute, and demons dread :

He craves to stand before an Altar, not a
 throne,
Bearing not the world's lordship, but its
 LORD !
And close the glories of his race thus glori-
 ously !
Ah ! his vocation is undoubted—but you—
FITZROI—Hear me, Lord Abbot ! when I first
 Heard you preach, after Evangeline had left me,
 I could sooner shut time into a den,
 Or steal eternity, to stop his glass,
 Than shut out the sweet ideas you then
  raised in me :
 I would retire into their contemplation.
 My lands, I will deliver them to you,
 Take them, and take my worthless self :
 Only your happy self, and those like you,
 Live out the larger, and the higher life :
 O let me have a part in it, for GOD's dear love !
 That GOD, without Whom e'en thou art
  nothing,
   With Him worthiest.

ABBOT—Your wish to take our Order seems
    sincere.
FITZBOI—My lord it is, although I am
    Circled and bound about with sins as many
    As in the house of memory live figures ;
    Let me soon kneeling, at thy feet, my faults
    Confess ; then rise a new man, and to a new
        life,
    That I may indue my Probation robe
    With an unburdened heart, and purified.
ABBOT—Remember, to such direction
    As the severity of the Monastic Life
    Deserves to lead your wisdom, and your
        judgment,
    You ought to yield obedience
    With assurance of will, and thankfulness,
        and manly courage.
    And to your submission as Probationer,
    You must add privacy, as strong in silence
    As mysteries locked up in GOD's own bosom :
    A skull hid in the earth a treble age,
    Shall sooner prate than any of my Monks.

FITZROI—I'll lay to heart what you have said.

ABBOT—As to the three great Vows—

FITZROI (*interrupting him, and raising his hand to Heaven*)—To Heaven, and all the bench of Saints above,

Whose succour I implore to enable me;
I vow henceforth a chaste life; not to enjoy
Anything proper to myself; obedience
To my Superior; the ground I tread upon
Is levell'd with the pleasures once held dear.

ABBOT (*rising*)—My business urging on a present haste,

Enforceth short reply.   I dare not hinder
Your resolution wing'd with thoughts so constant:
I love, and prize the deep strong will in you,
To work the thing that GOD hath called you to.

But—

FITZROI (*interrupts him*)—O let there be no buts;
You say that He has called me; I must come.
Upon my knees (*kneels*). I ask your pardon

For my rude boldness; let me be blest. I will
Not damp the expectations of your hopes,
And when I fail these hopes, Heaven's hopes
    fail me !
Ten years ago you brought my frightened
    faith
Home to my heart again; in token of my
    gratitude
Let me lay down my life under your sacred
    feet
To do God's service.
And when I fall from duty in my Calling,
May everlasting misery then find me !
Abbot—I do believe you :
You may come with your son, and then
    receive
The Scapulaire, the yoke of Him, that
Makes it sweet and light ; in which
Thy soul find her eternal rest.
       [*The* Abbot *blesses* Fitzroi *and Exit.*
Fitzroi—Am I awake, or dream I ?
Or does my flattering fancy but suggest

H

What most I covet?
The Scapulaire for me! so soon!
Heaven my helper, he never shall repent
  giving it to me.
Receive my thanks O GOD—
My tears must speak for me, my tongue
  cannot.   [*He prostrates himself.*

SCENE 17.

The Arch-Monastery.—The Monastery Garden.—
  CLAUDE, *a Monk, and* DUNSTAN, *a young*
  Postulant, walking in it.

CLAUDE—Such is the routine of our daily life:
  Our festivals are spent in mirth, and serious
    talk, and prayer;
  On those days we may speak till sounds the
    Compline bell;

Then two by two we wend into the Church,
O'er it we hear an Angel-choir singing
" Venite Sancti ! "   Entering soon are said
The psalm, " He giveth sleep," and hymn
  " Lætare ; "
We then retire to our cells, rejoicing in GOD'S
  love.
DUNSTAN—A blessed life! I long to take my
  part in it.
Tell me now something of my future Brothers.
[*Two rough, ungainly-looking Monks pass them.*
CLAUDE—These are our herdsmen, James and
  John ;
James plays as well, almost, as our chief
  organist, Fitzroi ;
John has the finest bass in all our choir.
DUNSTAN—You much surprise me. I would have
Sworn their souls were far from music,
And that all their choice music was to hear,
  Their fat beasts bellow.
CLAUDE—I was as much deceived in them at
  first ;

But they're the men indeed that hide their
    gifts,
And set them not to sale in every presence :
Pure virgin gold encased in pudding-stone.
DUNSTAN—Who is that dark and Roman-
    featured Monk ?
CLAUDE—That's George, he came with Fitzroi,
    and he is our poet.
Oh had you heard that song of his, John sang
To us last night ! " Let there be light," was
    ever the refrain :
Cuthbert was so delighted with it that he
    wept.
You've not seen Cuthbert yet—
He seldom comes to recreation ;
And, by how much the labours of the mind
Exceed the body, so far is he bound
With pain and industry, beyond the toil
Of those that sweat in war ; beyond the toil
Of any artisan : you'll know him
By his pale cheek, and by his sunken eye ;
His hair turned white in youth.

DUNSTAN—What is your department?

CLAUDE—I am the artist of the Monastery.

DUNSTAN—You did not paint those frescoes in
the Chapel!

CLAUDE—Why yes, of course I did.

DUNSTAN—They are of wondrous beauty.

CLAUDE—I'm glad they meet with your ap-
proval.

DUNSTAN—I can't conceal my wish to know
more of

A man who's made me feel and think so
much.

Thou hast strong sympathies,

Else how could sacred friendship touch thy
soul.

CLAUDE—Pity the wretch whose soul it never
touched!

And now I'll gratify your wish, as far as it
is right.

Ten years ago my father died: you've heard,

When the poor turtle's ravished from her
mate

The lonely dove doth moan away her life :
And so my mother lived in widowed solitude
A year ; then died after a brief illness, and
    belied
The report which says, that women vie with
    the
Nine Muses, for nine tough, durable.lives :
Since her death I have been in the Army ;
Doctor of Divinity, and of Medicine too,
And in that last line might have shone.
DUNSTAN—Your skill is spoke of all the country
    round.
CLAUDE—O contemptible physic ! that dost take
So long a study only to preserve so short a
    life :
This (*looking at his Discipline*) is the only
    leech that draws the bad blood out.
Tiring of medicine, I hunted after pleasure ;
Till I grew sick, and fell into deep thought :
My dear friend Tom, begged for my confi-
    dence,
By memories of the past, but I coldly said :

" To prate were idle ; I remember nothing :"
(O would I might recall those heartless
    words !
For he to whom I said them is now dead.
Dear Tom ! he had an honest heart, altho'
In form uglier than an unshaped bear.)
And then I fled by night, and I came here,
With my poor limb corrupted to an ulcer ;
But I have cut it off ;* and now I'll go
Weeping to Heaven on crutches.

DUNSTAN—What made you make your mind up
    to come here ?

CLAUDE—A dream determined me.
I dreamed that I was what I was, a slave,
Trampled by passion's hoof ; and that the
    Devil
Stood regarding me ; I turned to him and
    said :
" Love for my cousin gives my life no rest,

---

* " If thy hand or thy foot offend thee, cut them off and cast them
from thee ; it is better for thee to enter into life halt or maimed,
rather than having two hands or two feet to be cast into everlasting
fire."—Matt. xviii., 8, 9 ; Matt. v., 29, 30 ; Mark ix, 43, 45, 47.

My heart an Etna is within my breast—
Give me Scholastique, and my soul is yours."
DUNSTAN—What! are you our Abbot's cousin!
CLAUDE—I am: but hear my dream. "These
        words
Which you have uttered sign," the Devil said:
"And she is yours; the ink wherewith you
        write
Them must be blood." I pricked my left arm
        with my
Dagger's point, and wrote the words;
Scarce had I signed my name, than the figure
        of
Scholastique appeared, all covered with her
        cloak:
I went to her, and said: "Thou hast cost me
        my soul,
Yet not so dear has been the purchase, since
So glorious is the gain." I spoke, and gently
Drew aside her cloak, and discovered a
        skeleton—
The ghastly image said: "The Devil keeps

His promise in this way : and such are all
The pleasures and the glories of the world,
That you so covet." I shuddered, and awoke ;
And by the sufferings of the souls in Hell
I swore to be a Monk.
DUNSTAN—After such an awful dream
You had no other choice.
And were you unmolested by your friends ?
CLAUDE—Oh, no : for even Tom would say :
" Why veil your wondrous talents
Amid the sameness of obscurity ?
Go, show them forth, and let the world admire,
And praise the GOD who gifts a creature
    thus."
But when I told him of my vision,
He tempted me no more.
DUNSTAN—What was your vision ?
CLAUDE—I saw my mother ; she clasped me once
    again
To her pure heart, and said : " Go hide your
    gifts,
Go, hide them in the Bosom of thy GOD ! "

Sweet mother ! that far distant voice I hear,.
And passing out of youth, and out of time,
I would not turn at last and disobey.
DUNSTAN—Then you are tempted still ?
CLAUDE—I am, by my perverse desires.
DUNSTAN—And you want something that you
    have not got ?
CLAUDE—O, no ! there's no room for a wish,
But to continue still this Blessing to me.
DUNSTAN—Why are you tempted then to go
    back to the world ?
CLAUDE—Because at times I'm mad.
    Alas ! had my soul ne'er embraced
    The Phantom of earth's loveliness,
    This would not be.   *[He sighs.*
DUNSTAN—Your sadness grieves me.
CLAUDE—Dunstan, I would not be without it,—
This sweet, vast swell of melancholy,
O'er which my spirit broods alone, bears me
    from earth,
And purifies my chastened soul for Heaven.
                        [After a pause.

What makes me speak so openly to you,
I, who am so reserved !

DUNSTAN—Nor can I explain what draws me
So to you.

CLAUDE—It cheers me much to see a boy like you,
Giving up all for GOD.
Who falls for love of GOD shall rise a star.

DUNSTAN—I've nothing to give up ;
I've nothing to fall from ;
(*Bitterly*) I was a beggar born.

CLAUDE—Poverty is the gift of GOD, as well as
riches ;
And therefore do not speak with scorn of it.

DUNSTAN—I feel no scorn, but pity and deep love,
For that large class to which I belong,
The impoverished, and suffering,
Whom the Kingdom of this World does not
own.

CLAUDE—But to whom a Will and Testament
Not to be disputed, has bequeathed the King-
dom of Heaven.
Your parents then were poor ?

DUNSTAN (*blushing*)—I am the child of lowliness
    and vice,
    And happy only in my ignorance
    Of marks to show from whom, or whence I
    am.
    If this shall make me sink in your esteem,
    It will much trouble me.
CLAUDE—If I should say I loved you less,
    I should do that I never durst do—lie.
    But how did you come here?
DUNSTAN—Years sixteen are gone by on next
    St. Dunstan's Day, since in the Minster-Portal
    I was found, a sleeping infant; the Monks
    Took me up, and did with care sustain
    My helpless infancy; left not my childhood
    Without instruction; and they taught me
    things
    Which my soul treasured as its dearest wealth.
CLAUDE—Then you have lived with Monks
    before?
DUNSTAN—I did not live with them though I
    went to their school:

I was boarded with a Protégé of Abbess
Scholastique,
Her name is Rose, and she lives near the
Sacred Heart :
She's long past youth, and lost her children
and her husband; her last child died
about the time that I was brought to
her. In spite of poverty and trouble,
she has a strong love for the bright and
beautiful, therefore she loves the Angels.
But Brother 'ere the bell for Compline sounds,
Tell me something of our Abbot.
I'm told that you walked out with him to-day.
CLAUDE—I did ; I went with him to visit a poor
man who had just lost his only son.
Poor fellow ! in the wildness of his grief,
he said: "Why has the LORD thus
punished me ? what harm have ever I
done Him ? "
" 'Tis your rebellious will, not GOD afflicts you;
Will you, because your boy is ta'en to Para-
dise,

Find fault with GOD !" the Abbot said; the
 poor man murmured : "O Father bear
 with me ! My heart is very full."—
"Away with all that hides you from your-
 self ;
Your heart indeed is full, but witness Heaven!
Your sorrow, not GOD's love, fills up your
 heart.
Look up ; look at the Cross, my Son !"
The Abbot blending thus entreaty with re-
 proach,
Shed from his large dark eyes a shower of
 tears :
The poor man looking up, could now descry
That kingly brow, arched lofty for command,
And that heart-piercing smile.
" Father," he cried : " I will hereafter to my
 utmost strength
Study to be resigned."
As we came home, returning thro' the wood,
I touched upon the mystery of the Great
 Sacrament.

And he replied : " O ! I'll not ask, nor answer,
    how, or why— '
To meet my LORD; to know I have Him here,
Is knowing more than any circumstance
Or means by which I have Him : so much joy
Does not give leisure to reflect, or know,
Or trifle time in thinking.—
O Love ! Love ! Love !"—
A hideous yell ensued.
DUNSTAN—I heard that shriek prodigious,
    And had I not been in the Chapel,
    Keeping Watch, I should have joined
    The Brothers, who I heard all running out,
    To see what was the matter.
CLAUDE—It was the cry of Fiends tormented :
    Ill-pleased the Abbot saw them, and he raised
    The Staff of JESUS * up on high; howling,
        they fled.
    And then o'er all was silence : Soft fire lit
    The upturned faces of the Monks, that shone
        because

* The Crozier.

They gazed on Heaven by Angel faces
   thronged,
And answered light with light.
Then rang with hymns of Angels and of men,
That wood once Demon-haunted ;
And when it was ended—that wondrous
   strain—
Invisible myriads breathed : " Amen, Amen !"'
DUNSTAN—I heard your voices sounding like
   throbbing flood
That swells all night until it overflows.
                  [After a pause.
Does the Abbot ever join the Monks at recre-
   ation ?
CLAUDE—Sometimes, and when he does, another·
Air breathes through the room.
The old Monks, and the young behold him
With intensest gaze ; these feel more chas-
   tened joy :
They more profound repose.   I cannot blame
The youthful Postulants who watch
Upon the mat what rush will last arise

From his foot's pressure, 'ere the door is
    closed.
And when they sit at table, their obedient eyes
Will dwell on his, as though they are not
    well,
Unless they look where he looks.
DUNSTAN—Who is the Master of the Postulants ?
CLAUDE—Maur is the Master of the Novices,
    And also of the Postulants.
He is of humble parents born, if humble may
    be said
Of those who left behind a heritage of vir-
    tues.
And both were reft of life for the dear faith,
When Maur was quite a child :
And then his uncle fled to Rome with him ;
There he was devoted to the Priesthood ;
And when he was of age, he saw the Pope,
    and from
His hands he gained those sacred powers
      The very Angels envy.
DUNSTAN—Is he in disposition, like the Abbot ?

CLAUDE—Whatever after ages bear, or give the
    name of worth to,
  Must, if compared to our great Abbot, be but
    as foils
    To set his glory off the brighter.
DUNSTAN—I've heard his manner often disap-
    points.
CLAUDE—His mien, his speech
  Are sweetly simple, and full oft deceive
  Those trivial mortals who seem always wise.
  But when the matter matches his great
    mind,
  The hero rises; in his piercing eye
  Sits observation; on each glance of thought
  Decision follows, as the thunderbolt pursues
    the flash!
  And when he preaches, oh! he gazes round
    as though
  He flung on each his boundless heart, and
    longed,
  As only such a heart can long, to help the
    helpless.

DUNSTAN—I've heard him in the Minster preach:
  Not Angels with dread trumpets rending
    Heaven,
  And threat'ning final woe, could more appal
    the soul,
  Than death impenitent described by him.
  And yet he spoke with pity infinite, as though
  He would out of a good nature part with half
  His own whiteness to purge his fellows' stains.
  But I could never see him for the mighty
    throng.
      What is he like in person?
CLAUDE—He has a God-like presence: dignity
    and grace
  Adorn his frame, where manly beauty joins
      With strength herculean.
  His noble form seemed almost glorified
  The night I saw him when I ran from home;
  I saw him in the moonlight from the Abbey
    gate
  Emerge, and with the sign of office in his
    hand:

He saw me, he awaited me ; I knelt.
He hail'd me, " Peace be with you, cousin : "
    I replied :
" King of the Western world, be with you
    peace."
Rising, I went to him, and fell prostrate :
He said : " Fall not upon thy face, some
    thorn
May scratch it, foolish youth ! rise up ; for
    shame
To grovel 'fore an earthly image thus."
" Pardon me, cousin," I replied : " surely
Stars, if composed of earth, yet still are stars,
And must be looked at with uplifted eyes."
Ah—since that happy moment, years have
    gone,
It makes me almost sad to think how many.
DUNSTAN—I do not think man would be happy,
       Unless he could regret :
And I confess, how, looking back, a thought
Has touched, and tuned, or rather thrill'd
    my heart,

Too soft for sorrow, and too strong for joy.
CLAUDE—What! you a boy scarce sixteen years
of age—
[*The Compline-bell strikes, and they both go in.*

SCENE 18.

Monastery- Garden.—CLAUDE *and* DUNSTAN
walking in it.

DUNSTAN—The Abbot has been absent longer
than he said.
CLAUDE—I fear some serious matter keeps him:
I trust no harm has come to our brave Mis-
sion brothers.
DUNSTAN—Remember, if they are made Martyrs
of,
We must take up their work.
CLAUDE—Most willingly, with our Superior's
leave.

,But, Dunstan, you must not relax the Rule,
    Because the Abbot is away.

DUNSTAN—Have I done so ?

CLAUDE—Yes, once to-day you spoke to me in
    silence-time ;
You'll get yourself in trouble, and me too.

DUNSTAN—Ah, so I did; for I did want so much
    to know why you sometimes gaze with
    reverence on these young Monks, Cuth-
    bert and Sebastian.

CLAUDE—Because Sebastian has seen the Holy
    Grail ; *
And Cuthbert has saved his friend from Hell.

DUNSTAN—You speak symbolically ?

CLAUDE—I speak the simple truth.
    Some years ago, when I was walking with
    the Abbot
In the wood, we heard distinctly Demons speak:
" What shall we do ? " said one : " If we lose
    souls from

* The San Greal or Holy Grail, was the Cup out of which JESUS
partook of the last Supper with His disciples.

Hell like this, we may soon shut up shop:
He's got Alexius from us—Cuthbert has."
"How did he get him?" howled out then
   the other.
" Could Hell not stop his prayers from enter-
   ing Heaven?"
" No, devil-brother, not such prayers, they
   beat
At all the windows of the highest Heaven,
And brake thro' all the brazen gates of Hell;
Alexius is now on his way to Paradise—
But Cuthbert knows not yet his great success:
Hark! to the fool, hear how he prays again."
Then thro' the dead-still silence of the night,
We heard from Cuthbert's open window-cell
   these words :
" O GOD; though Pagan, love within him
   dwells ; therefore
Not his that doom of souls, all hate and wil-
   ful blind;
To whom Thy presence were a woe untold.
Eternal pity ! pity him—Alexius.

Sole Peace of them that love Thee, grant him
    peace.
O more than peace, the rapturous vision
Of the Face of GOD, won by the Cross of
    CHRIST."

*   *   *   *   *   *   *   *

[ROMANUS *comes quickly into the Garden,*
    and whispers CLAUDE, *and they both*
    hasten into the Church, followed by DUN-
.   STAN : *they enter a side Chapel, dedicated*
    to All Saints, and PLACIDUS *is seen lying*
    before the Shrine in the form of a Cross.

CLAUDE—And did he speak at first ?
ROMANUS—He said : "I come," and I thought
    sighed.
I do not like his staying when Maur bid
    him come ;
I never knew him fail, for were it fire,
And that fire certain to consume his body,
If his Superior sent, he would be sure to go.

CLAUDE—He's rapt in his devotions, but we
must rouse him.
[*They go up to* PLACIDUS, *and* CLAUDE *bends over*
him and calls into his ear.
Your watch
Is past, and Maur has sent for you.
DUNSTAN—He still is prostrate, and I think he
sleeps.
ROMANUS—How fast he is! I cannot hear him
breathe.
CLAUDE—Gently raise his head—so . . .
ROMANUS—Either the tapers give a feeble light,
Or he looks very pale.
DUNSTAN—And so he does; pray Heaven he be
well.
ROMANUS—O GOD, if he is gone!
CLAUDE (*putting* ROMANUS *and* DUNSTAN *aside*)—
Let's look . . . . Alas! he's dead.
The rapture of repose on his pale lips appears!
Could any one hate death, and see it here?
DUNSTAN—Methinks to die so were to ascend
To Heaven thro' Paradise.

[*As they are preparing to take the body away,*
     MAUR *enters and motions them to leave it*
     where it is, and to go out.—Exeunt
     ROMANUS, CLAUDE, *and* DUNSTAN.

MAUR (*kneeling by the body*)—O Brother, Unpro-
     fessed, yet well beloved !

   Though for certain reasons, there wanted that
   Which often keeps poor mortals in great awe
   From starting from their vow, the knot public,
   'Twas in your soul knit fast; and how more
     precious
   The soul is than the body, so much I judge
   The sacred and celestial tie within you,
   More than the outward form, which calls but
     witness
   Here upon earth, to what is done in Heaven.
   And must I yield thee thus ? for ever thus . .
   I have no power, except to love thee still.

[*Rising after a few minutes, and placing his*
     hand on the head of PLACIDUS.

   Farewell Placidus: placid were thy days
   Which flowed through blessings. As a river
     pure,

Whose sides are flow'ry, and whose meadows
    fair,
Meets in his course a subterranean void;
There dips his silver head again to rise,
And rising, glide through flowers and
    meadows new,
So shall Placidus in those happier fields,
Where never gloom of trouble shades the
    mind.   [*Exit.*

SCENE 19.

The Arch-Monastery—Recreation-room.—CLAUDE
and DUNSTAN.

DUNSTAN—I cannot realise that we shall
    Never see Placidus again.
CLAUDE—His was a sudden call, but I had
    noticed for some time that his health
    was failing.
DUNSTAN—About four days ago,
    I met him i' the Cloister, and asked him

How he did ?   Taking me by the hand
He wrung it, and after a sigh or two, told me,
" Not very well," but Vespers rung, and so we
  parted.
CLAUDE—Did you mark when we were praying
  round his Corpse,
It shone with other light than the still stars
Shed on its rest, or the dim tapers nigh ?
DUNSTAN—I did; and also when Maur
Called him good and happy,
Methought his Corpse smiled faintly thro' the
  ⁻ quiet gloom.
CLAUDE—Brother, I could have sworn it—
And that his haircloth throbb'd upon his
  grateful heart.
DUNSTAN—Dear Placidus, whose innocence
      The Saints were pleased with.
CLAUDE—And offering at their Altar, gave his
  soul.
DUNSTAN—What is he doing now think you ?
CLAUDE—Perhaps he helps to swell the Liturgy
  of hallowed Pain.

O Brother ! who would not break away if he
    could,
From this body, and fly to the lowest place in
That most pure, most safe, most silent land of
Suffering, and sinless love !
DUNSTAN—But by this time, I think he's got to
    Paradise ;
And is now lifting up love-large eyes dilated
By great destinies. Thrones, and Seraphim,
Sunning him with sweet looks of Heaven's
    delight.
CLAUDE—It may be so : for if ever
Heaven's high blessing met in one man,
And there erected to their holy uses
A sacred mind fit for their services—
'Twas in Placidus.
DUNSTAN—There was about him an atmosphere of
Unearthly calmness ; his human will seem'd
Almost without human activity.
CLAUDE—It lay still in the lap of the will of GOD.
DUNSTAN—In that respect he was like our dear
    LORD.

CLAUDE—Yes : for the eagerness, the passionate
    desire,
To shed His Blood, stands quite alone
In our LORD's life of three-and-thirty years :
With desire had He desired to communicate
With His chosen few in the Blessed Sacrifice,
Wherein His Blood is mystically shed.
He bedewed the ground at Gethsemane
With priceless drops, as if He could not wait
For the violence of Calvary.
DUNSTAN—Brother, I love to hear you ;
    It makes me forget myself.
CLAUDE—I think man's happiest when he forgets
    himself.
But what ails you ? you look haggard.
DUNSTAN—I am anxious about William, and
    Richard ; and have but broken rest—
And when I do sleep, only dream of them.
CLAUDE—What do you dream or fear ?
DUNSTAN—I dream of them in pain and suffering,
    I fear a violent death.
CLAUDE—If so, there is deep comfort

In associating the thought of them
With the remembrance of the unknown
    sufferings
Of our LORD, and giving them up to Him,
And to His dear Mother to be cared for.
    [*The Angelus sounds, and they both kneel.*

SCENE 20.

A Prison.—WILLIAM *in chains.*   *Enter* RICHARD,*
Guard in attendance.

RICHARD—What, in tears, my Brother?
WILLIAM—Think not these tears unnerve me,
    They have but harmonised my soul; and
        waked
    All that is man within me, to disdain

* Richard and William, Mission Monks. On hearing of their
danger, S. Benedict at once went to them, hoping to prevail with the
barbarous people into whose power they had fallen, to save their
lives; but his efforts were unavailing.

Torture or death.

Give me thy hand; I will not say, thou'rt
welcome;

That is the common road of common friends;

I'm glad I have thee here—oh! I want words

To let thee know my heart.

RICHARD—'Tis pieced to mine.

WILLIAM—Yes, 'tis; as firmly as that holy thing

Called Brotherhood can make it.

RICHARD—Well dearest Brother, 'tis at hand,

The hour our hearts forecast that night

We heard the roar of savage beasts.

WILLIAM—Full well I do remember me that
night,

Then felt I first the fear and hope,

That we might live to glut the fury

Of those wild deputies of cruel man.

How feel you now about to-morrow's fate?

RICHARD—I scarce believe it—

What have we done to merit such a grace!

WILLIAM—O Richard, can you grasp it;—

That we, shut up within these prison walls,

Ere sets that sun which brings to-morrow's
    light,
Shall see Him face to face.
RICHARD—To close our eyes on thousand hideous
    looks,
And on that bright Intelligence unclose them,
This shall be ours to-morrow—
                  [*Clock strikes twelve.*
Oh, to-day !
WILLIAM—O blessed day, which gives us to our
    LORD !
Whom we have seen, e'en thro' earth's mist,
    so beautiful ;
Whom we have loved, distant yet near ;
    In whom
Our souls have trusted, and our hearts
    rejoiced :
Come, LORD, come quickly !
RICHARD—And the good Abbot, from whose
    words
Our hearts have sucked the Christian Faith ;
Who marked us as our SAVIOUR's Own ;

And kept us in the way when we would
    fall—*

He will be near us at the dreadful end.

How like his love to that which GOD hath
    borne us !

WILLIAM—He'll touch our lips when we can speak
    no more,

With the dear sign of Him who died for us.

He's gone, Saint Benedict I mean—but he
    will soon return

To hear my last Confession. Farewell, fare-
    well !

To meet again, and then to part—oh no !

And then to meet for ever.

[*They embrace. Enter the* ABBOT—RICHARD *and*
    WILLIAM *kneel.*

ABBOT—Why do they kneel ? ·Stand up ;

    My sons, this day and place is privileged.

---

* The parents of Richard and William were heathens, converted by
S. Benedict, who also baptised and instructed their children, and
brought them to the Arch-Monastery to be trained for Missionary
Monks. As soon as they were Professed, they returned to their native
land, in order to teach their countrymen the true faith; and there
met with the Martyrs' fate.

WILLIAM—Father, your presence makes this
  prison cell a Sanctuary.

ABBOT—Use not such reverence in duty to me
  now :

Rise ! 'tis I should kneel to you ;

To call you Sons, to hear you call me Father,

I feel it is an honour, that a sinner

Cannot but entertain with thankful prayers.

RICHARD—Father, bear us in mind where prayer
  is ever heard,

Blent with the Bloodless Sacrifice.

ABBOT—Whose Blood gives Martyrs' blood the
  tongue to plead

For sinners pardon, and the Church's rest.

WILLIAM—Thanks be to GOD !

ABBOT—You shall not kneel to us ;

Rise both, I charge you.

      [*Gazing intently upon them.*

Well, I'll kneel, too ; and may these holy
  thoughts

That now possess us wholly, make this place

A temple to me where I may give thanks

For blessings undeserved, Heaven's kind hand
Hath poured upon me in giving me such
   children !
[*Silence for a few minutes,* then the ABBOT *rises.*
ABBOT—My children, best beloved ! with you
My task is o'er, GOD's glory consummate ;
And what have I to do, but leave the work
With Him who hath disposed it ?
Thanks to my LORD and KING !
Thanks, thanks for ever !

               [*Exeunt* RICHARD *and* GUARD.

SCENE 21.

Garden of the Arch-Monastery.—CLAUDE *and*
DUNSTAN.

CLAUDE—Brother, 'twas not unkindness made
   me start away,
When I last met you in the Cloisters ;

But I had just then heard of our brave
    Martyrs' death,
And wished to deal with bitter grief alone.
DUNSTAN—Richard and William killed?
Not both?
CLAUDE—Both, both, my Brother.
    Here, read this letter, it will tell you all.
                    [Gives him a letter and is going.
DUNSTAN—Stay till I have read the letter.
CLAUDE—I may not, as I am attending on the
    Abbot.
DUNSTAN—How does the Abbot?
CLAUDE—Sleeps still.
DUNSTAN—When you can, come hither, and
    Tell what more thou knowest.
CLAUDE—I will.
                          [Exit.

SCENE 22.

Three Angels.—(1) GUARDIAN *of the Arch-Monastery.* (2) GUARDIAN *of Abbess Scholastique.* (3) ANGEL *of Death.*

———

(2) ANGEL—Deep in the councils of the Monastery
Thou art; what's the news from thence
Worthy to take to Heaven?

(1) ANGEL—The Martyrs' death.

(2) ANGEL—Ah yes, the Abbess told me of it;
Brother, I do not grieve; there is a special sweetness
In the thought of death.

(3) ANGEL—O friend! 'tis a pleasant fable unto you,
Who know it but in fancy, wreathed in flowers,
And sung in solemn hymns, and ornamented
With glorious legends, as the Martyrs' fate;

Old age's refuge, and the crowning choice
    Of virtue in extremity.
It is impossible for me to know a touch of
    pain,
And yet, I feel an awful something when I see
The agonizing wrench of soul from flesh ;
I hold two passions in my soul at once,
Of gladness and of sorrow.
(1) ANGEL—How did the Martyrs die ?
(3) ANGEL—'Twas early morn when Benedict—
(1) ANGEL—Blest Benedict,
    To whose memory my heart does dedicate
Itself an altar, in whose very mention
My lips are hallowed, and the place a temple
Whence the Divine sound came ; it is a voice
Which should the holy Churchmen use, it
    might
Without addition of more exorcism
Disenchant houses, tie up wicked spirits :
Saint Benedict when I have named, I needs
Must love my breath the better after it.
Forgive this interruption.

(3) ANGEL—It needs no excuse.
    Saint Benedict was kneeling by the Martyrs'
        side,
    When a roar as of a myriad thunders burst—
    And low the lion cower'd in act to spring :
    And then the soul of silence reigned, and
        breath
    Thro' the ten thousand pallid lips, unfelt,
    Stole from the stricken bosoms :
    Rudely the Saintly Abbot was thrust back.

      *   *   *   *   *   *

    Richard and William were alone; they stood,
    With face uplifted, and eyes fixed on air,
    Which unto them was thronged with Angel-
        forms :
    Then Silence, veil of terrible repose,
    Lifted its folds to glare on agony;
    One dreadful glance sufficed—all was over—
    The heartless crowd pressed out.
    And thro' an Arch-triumphal, formed of
        Cherubim,

The Conquerors pressed in to the Unspoken
　　Raptures.
And there was one—the Abbot—who went
　　up to their
Poor mutilated bodies ;* and kneeling down,
With his pale patient face lifted towards
Heaven, itself sufficient prayer—thanked GOD.
.(2) ANGEL—Where do their bodies rest ?
(1) ANGEL—One grave received them in the
　　Cloister's Cemetery.
(Healing thence to many from their relics
　　pass ; to more
The spirit's happier healing, love and faith.)
One Cross is at its head, o'ershadowed by the
　　palm,
Because their hearts were one, and one their
　　lives :
And every morning with fresh flowers their
　　grave
Is covered, white violets, palm leaves, and
　　lilies newly open'd :

* The wild beasts would not touch their bodies after death.

O'er it the snowy-breasted bird of ocean oft'
    flies
With wailing note : but they rejoice
'Mid GOD's High Realm, glittering in endless
    youth.
(3) ANGEL—May their prayers for sinners plead !
(2) ANGEL—Last night the Abbess dreamed
    Her soul was mounted up into the highest
        Heaven,
    And there she saw Richard and William both
    Enthroned, and backed with a troop of fiery
        Cherubims,
    Dancing about their newly-healed wounds,
    Singing sweet hymns, and chanting heavenly
        notes ;
    Rare harmony to greet their innocence.
(1) ANGEL—Thou hast a precious Charge.
(2) ANGEL—O ! when I think what pleasure I
        took in her
    Ere she could speak : what joy her glowing
        love
    For GOD gave me, and as she worshipped Him

How have I stood and fed my eyes upon her,
Then, lifting up my hands, and, wondering,
    blessed her—
I could talk of a thousand things at once,
And all of thee ; my Child, of thee ;
Hark ! she invokes me : thro' the vast distance
    I can feel
The supplication softly strong of eyes,
Like planets seen thro' mist !
I come ! my Child, I come !

                    [*Exeunt* ANGELS.

PART THIRD.

SCENE 23.

Monastery Garden.—CLAUDE *and* DUNSTAN.

DUNSTAN—How dared you lift your eyes to the
    Abbess ?

CLAUDE—She was not Abbess then ;

It was when we last gathered roses in the
    garden of the Castle :

She was a girl, and I almost a boy.

(*sadly*) Some men can never come to aim at
    Heaven

But by the knowledge of a Hell :

You, who as chaste as wind-fan'd snow, and
    will be so,

Not only in your eastern days* but in your
    western, too ;

---

* Pure in his early as well in his declining years.

You who alone love GOD, and whose soul
Is loosened from your senses, cannot judge
What torments mine of grosser mould endured,
When she replied: "Dear Claude, hope
    greater things;
But hope not this; haste to overcome your
    love;
It is but putting a short-lived passion to a
    violent death:
For me all love is lust, but love of HEAVEN;
Nor can I keep vacated heart-space for an
    alien care."
DUNSTAN—She was not angry then?
CLAUDE—No, that emboldened me to take her
    hand;
I know not what I said; wild words, and
    miserable.
In sorrow more than anger, she withdrew
Her hand from mine, and looking up, she
    sighed, and prayed:
"O HEAVEN, protect his weakness with Thy
    strength!

Banish his earthy spirit, O Great God !
Transform him from this flesh, that he may
    live,
·Before his death, regenerate with Thee:
That when he thinks, Thy thoughts may be
    his guide,
And, when he speaks, he may be made by
    choice
The perfect echo of Thy heavenly voice."
DUNSTAN—It was a grand prayer, and beautiful;
    And faithfully was answered ;
    GOD caught the words, and hid them in His
        heart,
    As night the stars.
CLAUDE—And as she prayed, she did shed . . .
    Tears I will not say . . . a tear : . .
    Shed it ! no ; I am wrong : it came, it stayed,
    As hangs one star, the first and only one,
    Twinkling, upon some vernal eve.
DUNSTAN—And could you speak ?
CLAUDE—I faltered out : " Farewell ! even vic-
        tory,

Glad as it is, must lend some tears to thee;
Many I dare not shed, lest you believe
I joy in you less than for you I grieve."
DUNSTAN—And then she left you?
CLAUDE—She did: and then, I fainted.
DUNSTAN—Poor Claude! yet it was best for both.
CLAUDE—It was: henceforth we gaze upon each
    other,
As the two Cherubims upon the Ark;
The living GOD between.
[An old Monk passes CLAUDE and DUNSTAN, and
    goes into the Monastery—DUNSTAN looking
    after him.
Brother who is that man?
What grandeur in his carriage, and his form!
CLAUDE—Why, you know Lucian; he was the
    first
Monk here—You've often seen him.*
DUNSTAN—It may be so, but until now I've not
Perceived his look of majesty and suffering;

---

* Lucian was one of the rebel angels who repented, and asked to
be forgiven, and was sent to earth to expiate his guilt.

Altho' I've heard he has by dreadful absti-
nence,
Deep contemplation, and unwearied study,
In years outstretched beyond the date of man,.
Attained to sovereignty over those deep
And secret things, which others fear and
know not.
Don't you think he's somewhat like our Ber--
nard ?
CLAUDE—Like, yet unlike, the self-same almost
Awful dignity of bearing ; but Bernard's
Graceful and serene, and happiness itself :
I once saw him when he was sleeping, and
His expression was so beautiful and bright,
That his sleep seemed less slumber than.
Paradise.
DUNSTAN—Yet Bernard, I can understand—
But Lucian ? Where does he come from ?
CLAUDE—The Abbot only knows from whence
he came :
He seems for power and splendid honour
framed ;

Rich is his mind in every art divine;
Through ev'ry path of science has he walked,
The votary of wisdom : we nothing know,
But yet we all agree, he is a mystery
Immersed in sadness, and of royal birth.
We must go in, for here he comes again,
Conversing with the Abbot.

                   [CLAUDE *and* DUNSTAN *go in.*

LUCIAN—Mine own remembrance is a misery
Too mighty for me, and keeps night here;

                   [*Strikes his breast.*

And throws an unknown wilderness about
     me :
And could the LORD again restore my
     credit,
As fair and absolute as first I had it,
I should not trust myself again.

ABBOT—I almost glory in your penitence :
But finish your strange tale.

LUCIAN—Where was I ?

ABBOT—You had left the Rebels, and were trying
     to retrace your steps.

LUCIAN—But instead of retracing them, I
      seemed to pitch headlong down an abyss:
I remember no more.
ABBOT—Where was your soul during those
      countless ages?
LUCIAN—Brother, I cannot tell.
Whatever she saw, or wherever she travelled
In her trance, she kept her own secret;
No word to memory did she whisper;
And baffled all imagination
By silence indissoluble.
I only know that consciousness revived
In fear, as in a racking sort of strife
I entered this sad prison (*beats his breast*) with
      a groan,
And a long, long shiver, and looking up I
      saw
The porch of a great building near,
To which I dragged myself.
ABBOT—The Arch-Monastery gate?
LUCIAN—It was. You and Maur carried me
      into the house;

I stared at you, helpless, and wondering
Into what regions, and amongst what beings
I was waking.

ABBOT—Our ways must seem to you but coarse,
After the blaze, the splendour and the sym-
metry
Of the pure fanes above.

LUCIAN—It is not that which troubles me;
It is that I am unforgiven:
Last night I had a fallen-angel's dream;
All Heaven within that hour was mine—
Brother, I was forgiven.

ABBOT (*clapping his hand on* LUCIAN)—Angel,
thou art;
And GOD has bid me say to thee,
That on our next and greatest festive day
Thou shalt escape, and be for ever ta'en
Into the gentle bosom of His love.

LUCIAN—Thanks be to GOD!

            [*He prostrates himself.*

SCENE 24.

Arch-Monastery.—Eastermorn, a little before day-
*break.—*CLAUDE's *Cell:* CLAUDE *lies on his*
pallet in religious dress, asleep, but restless:
ROMANUS *comes in and looks at him.*

———

CLAUDE (*in his sleep*)—Trouble thy repose!
   Scholastique!
ROMANUS (*gently shakes him*)—Hush! hush!
   My brother, for the LORD has risen.
               [CLAUDE *looks wildly about him.*
ROMANUS—You have been dreaming?
CLAUDE (*rising*)—I have had such a dream!
   Scholastique appeared to me in more than
      human beauty;
   I stood motionless; I feared to lose
   Anything attendant on her presence;
   I feared to touch the lily in her hand,
   Which filled my whole soul with fragrance:

I bowed my head at last to kiss her snow-
    white robe,
Trembling at my presumption :
She smiled, and her smile pierced me to the
    heart ;
It seemed an angel's. "Oh, my beloved!"
    said she :
" We have consigned to the Bosom of GOD
Our earthly joys and sorrows ;
The joys cannot return, let not the sorrows ;
These alone would trouble my repose
Among the Blessed." " Trouble thy re-
    pose !
Scholastique ! " I cried out : and awoke.
ROMANUS—It was more than a dream :
Last night Saint Raphael took Scholastique
    away.
Margaret is Abbess now.
Look up ! Scholastique is yonder, and waiting
    for thee.
CLAUDE (*looks up*)—I see the clear dawn break-
    ing—

ROMANUS—O look again, there's something
  brighter above it !

CLAUDE—There is . . . O great GOD !
 The LORD is risen indeed—

ROMANUS—And the mystical invitation has
  arrived

 For that true spouse of JESUS CHRIST :
 " Arise,

 Make haste and come; for the winter is now
  past,

 The rain is over and gone."

     [*Enter* DUNSTAN *pale and agitated.*

DUNSTAN—O Brothers, do you hear it !

[*As he speaks, a burst of triumphant music
 is wafted up from the Chapel.*

CLAUDE—'Tis " Lætabitur Justus ! "

ROMANUS—O Heaven ! What does it mean ?

DUNSTAN—Lucian has just been found dead on
  his knees.

 The Abbot saw him; and he dropped a tear
  and said :

 " Illustrious ruin ! May the grave impart

That peace which life denied !" Scarce had
These words escaped his lips, when lo !
A shout of Angels' music :
And I rushed from the Chapel, to bring there
The few that were not present.
Come, Brothers, come !

[*As* DUNSTAN, CLAUDE, *and* ROMANUS *are going
to the Chapel, the glorious music rises and
swells thro' the Arch-Monastery, and they
and all the other Monks, inspired, take
up the victorious strain. Scene closes.*

SCENE 25.

*Arch-Monastery—Recreation-room—Easter Mon-
day—*VICTOR, DUNSTAN, *and* CLAUDE.

VICTOR—'Tis known, the Brother Lucian's
death ;
I marked the people as they came from Mass,

In crowds assembled, and struck with silent sorrow,

And pouring forth the noblest praise—of tears!

DUNSTAN—What is that noise outside?

VICTOR—'Tis the poor people coming for their Easter blessing;

Just like a hive of bees they swarm up to the gates, and with

Confused cries, hinder themselves from being understood;

Till some having divers times cried: " The Abbot! " all with one note,

Make up a common voice, and so continue.

CLAUDE—What shall we do? the Abbot must not be disturbed,

For he has scarce returned from seeing the Abbess lying out in state.

DUNSTAN—Good GOD! the Abbess dead!

CLAUDE—Hush! Brother—only another Saint to plead for us above.

DUNSTAN (*aside*)—And can you speak of it so calmly?

CLAUDE (*aside*)—And could I not, I were unworthy of her love.

[*The people outside cry out for the* ABBOT.

CLAUDE (*aloud*)—Poor creatures; come, Dunstan

Let us go out and speak to them, and then,
When they are quiet, the Abbot will appear,
And give the Easter blessing :
Victor will stay and welcome our new Postulant.

VICTOR—Who is he ?

CLAUDE—I only know his name; 'tis Vincent.

VICTOR—That was my father's name.

[*Exeunt* CLAUDE *and* DUNSTAN.—*Enter* MAUR
with VINCENT, *a veteran of rank, and of a
noble, though sad countenance.*

MAUR—You join us on a blessed day,
Then wherefore look so sad ?

VINCENT—'Tis seven years to-day since I lost
my only son.

VICTOR (*aside*)—My father ! I could swear it.

[MAUR *takes* VINCENT *to* VICTOR.

MAUR (*laying his hand on* VICTOR's *head*)—Does
   this young Monk remind you of your
   son?

VINCENT—He does; strongly and strangely so.
               [*Turns and gazes at* VICTOR.
But you look older than my boy would be.

MAUR—His name is Victor.

VINCENT (*still gazing earnestly at* VICTOR)—'Tis
   not for your name's sake alone I love you;
'Tis not your shape, which yet hath so much
   sweetness,
Some praying hermit might suspect
You are the blessed Saint he has in special
   honour.
Mother of GOD! why do I love you so?

VICTOR—The magic's in our nature,
For both our veins full of one precious purple,
Strike harmony in their motions: I am your
   son.

VINCENT—Ah! Brother do not mock me, I am
   old, and weak.

MAUR—By GOD! he speaks the truth.

For seven revolving years, and five of that
    seven
Worn out in tedious exile, may have wrought
Such change of voice and feature in the
State of youth, as might elude thine eye.
VINCENT—No time can blot
The mark indelible, a beauteous scar,
Made on his forehead by a furious Goth,
Who rushing on me, my brave Victor slew.
MAUR—A scar !
VINCENT—Ay, on his forehead.
MAUR—What ! like this ? (*lifting* VICTOR's *cowl.*)

    ✽   ✽   ✽   ✽   ✽   ✽

VINCENT—Do I not dream ? do I behold this
    sight
With waking eyes ? or from the ivory gate
Hath Morpheus sent a vision to delude me ?
                [VICTOR *embraces him.*
VICTOR—My true-loved father ! Do I hold you
    fast,
Never to part again ? Can I believe it ?

VINCENT—Crack not yet, ye feeble ministers of
    Nature,
With inundation of such swelling joy.
There's more than life itself in dying here;
If I must fall, death's welcome in these arms.
            [*He faints in* VICTOR'S *arms.*

*   *   *   *   *   *

MAUR (*bathing his forehead and·hands*)—Excess
    of joy from seeing you,
Has overpowered him : I was to blame
To take his deep affection unprepared.
VICTOR—My dearest father !
VINCENT (*opening his eyes*)—Where have I been ?
Why do you keep him from me ?
I heard his voice : My life upon the wing,
There's the soft lure that brings me back
    again !
(*To* MAUR)—Pardon me Brother—
Excuse the wild disorder of my soul;
The strange, surprising joy of meeting Victor
    here,

Of seeing him again, distracted me.

(*To* VICTOR)—What hand of Providence has
    brought you here?

O tell me all, for every thought confounds me.

I thought you dead, killed at the dreadful
    Siege :

And then, I heard still worse, that you were
    living,

And had accepted office with the Goths.

Your *No* would soon have answered accusa-
    tion false,

Why then did you not speak it?

VICTOR—My lips were sealed by the example too
    sublime to name.

VINCENT—My brave boy still!

How did I lose you in that conflict desperate?

VICTOR—When did you last see me?

VINCENT—Heading a fearful charge.

VICTOR—And there I fell among the dead ;

    But hope of life reviving from my wounds,

    I was preserved, but to be made a slave.

    How I lived in bondage for five years ;

How I escaped from it; and how came here;
It would be tedious at this time to tell;
And you want rest.

VINCENT—I have a thousand things to say to
    thee.

MAUR—At leisure all to-morrow shall be told;
    But now I wait to take you to your cell:
    How are you Brother now ?*

VINCENT—I am; but how, I rather feel than
    know.   [*Exeunt.*

SCENE 26.

Monastery Woods.—VINCENT *and* VICTOR.

VINCENT—If we have time, do let us go
    To our good Abbot's cave, where he lived
    When a youth; and there composed his Rule
        inspired.

VICTOR—I fear it is too far for you.

* Postulants and Novices were called Brothers by courtesy.

VINCENT—I've set my heart on seeing it.

VICTOR—Come on then, take my arm;
And as we go, you'll recount your adventures;
For I have told you mine.

VINCENT (*leans on* VICTOR)—Few words will tell
you all:
After my hope of finding you was gone,
I suspended for ever over the Altar,
My helmet and my sword.

VICTOR—Why then did you not enter here
before?

VINCENT—The Abbot did not think till now
that
My Vocation was sufficiently defined:
'Twas Maur that spoke for me, and brought
me in;
And therefore he's my favourite 'mong the
Monks.

VICTOR—He's also mine. I do enjoy his
lectures so.

VINCENT—To-day I could not follow him in the
Distinctions to be observed between *Latria*
And *Dulia:* did you take up his meaning?

VICTOR—I think, I did: In the law of the
    Church, the word
    Latria signifies the worship due to GOD alone;
    In opposition to *Dulia*, which is given only
      to the Saints.
VINCENT—He promised to talk over it with me,
    Some evening in the Garden.
VICTOR—Ah! you've not seen our Garden yet.
VINCENT—Is it as wondrous fair as report says?
VICTOR—Yes; and its fragrant perfume,
    Clings to the very garments that we wear.
VINCENT—I fancy that I feel sweet fragrance
    Whene'er I pass the Monks;
    And that I feel it now from you.
VICTOR—It is no fancy, father:
    All our garments smell of myrrh, aloes, cassia.
VINCENT—I've heard that in your Garden,
    By the brief contact of the Abbot's feet,
    More flowers are born without the aid of time,
    Than April bears with all its labouring hours.
VICTOR—Flowers which wither not tho' culled,
    But on our Shrines, and on our Altar bloom,
    As in their native fields.

VINCENT—They caught my eye soon as I
    entered Chapel;
So gorgeous were their hues! gold and snow
In purple pomp were met, and put to shame
The colours of the rainbow arch.
VICTOR—I'll ask the Abbot's leave to let you see
The view from my cell's window.
VINCENT—Can you see much from it?
VICTOR—Yes, much of sky, and much of meadow,
    A wood, a rivulet, a mountain;
    But nearer than all these, the Monastery
        Garden,
    Where rich-plumed birds in rapturous song
        sweep by;
    And the harmony of plant and flower,
    In wild beauteous mazes mingle,
    Though so natural it seems,
    You must know 'tis artificial;
    For upon each lovely leaf,
    Rare devices Heaven has printed.
VINCENT—Oh, how I long to see it!
    Who are your gardeners?

M

VICTOR—The Monks take it in turn.

VINCENT—And did they plant these delicious
    woods

That we now walk in ?

VICTOR—They did; and with rich harvest
    clothed the hills

Of our rock-engirdled home.

VINCENT—Home . . . Victor have you no long-
    ing

To see once more the home of your child-
    hood ?

VICTOR—Father, not now, and yet I love the
    very stones

Of that dear house, with the marks upon the
    door,

To show my growth at every birthday since
    my first.

VINCENT—Ah, you have no regrets : but I . . .

When I pass along the meditative Cloisters,

Deep recollections of the past delay my pro-
    gress.

Ah ! dear departed days ; where are ye gone?

VICTOR—Father! you do not wish them back?

VINCENT—Oh, no! only . . . GOD's Mother!
 I turn child.

VICTOR—What! tears—   [*Weeps.*

VINCENT—In this short moment that I live, I
 have whate'er the longest life could give.

Let me weep away a part of too much happiness.

To think that all my grief should end thus . .
 thus—

O Victor! I've remained so strictly bound to
 sorrow

For thy loss, that nothing else, tho' never so
 befitting,

Obtained my care, or observation.

VICTOR—Lean on me more; your weakness
 troubles me.

VINCENT—Is it far now to our good Abbot's
 cave?

VICTOR—About a mile.

VINCENT—Ah, then I cannot go; my breathing
 is too bad.

We'll rest a little; and you'll describe the
    cave.

                                    [*They sit down.*
VICTOR—'Tis sheltered by a hill,*
    Whose pointed crags are soften'd to the sight
            By figs and grapes.
O'er half the entrance, downward from the
    roots,
Nature has hung the shaggy trunks of firs,
To Heaven's hot rays impervious. Near the
    mouth
Relucent laurels spread before the sun
A broad and vivid foliage. High above
The hill is darken'd by a solemn shade,
Diffused from ancient cedars; the front
Looks on a crystal pool, by feathered tribes
At every dawn frequented: from the springs
A rippling brook breaks silence, and entices
        The ear of night to listen undisturbed.
It is unchanged since the Saint lived in it.

---

* Romanus describes the cave from a different aspect (see page 12).
—Both descriptions are correct.

VINCENT—I see it plain, that blessed cave.
Thanks, honour of my drooping age,
For Victor, I am drooping;
My life-glass sands are almost spent:
And now I feel as I ne'er felt before, that
Glories of human greatness are but pleasing
    dreams,
And shadows soon decaying: on the stage
Of my mortality my youth hath acted
Some scenes of vanity, drawn out at length
By varied pleasures, sweeten'd in the mixture,
    But happiest at the close.
VICTOR—Father, you're looking weary;
Shall we go in?   [*Offers to go.*
VINCENT (*catching hold of his arm*)—A moment!
    give me yet a moment's space,
To tell you Victor you must promise to convey,
(Ere I die, as a last act of kindness;)
My expiring body to the spot you have
So well described; mind, that it is my wish,
My struggling spirit take from earth
Its latest flight from thence.

VICTOR (*moved*)—My honoured father !

VINCENT—See the moon rises o'er the everlast-
    ing hills !
How strikingly the course of nature tells,
By its light heed of human suffering,
That it was fashion'd for a happier world.
        Let us return.

[*They rise and walk towards the Monastery; as
    they approach it,* VINCENT *stands for a
    minute, and looks up at the building.*

VINCENT—How reverend is the face of that
    vast pile,
        Looking tranquillity !
I see a figure in the topmost turret.

VICTOR—It is the Abbot; and he can see
From thence the greatest cities of the world ;
So marvellously extensive is the view.
Yesterday he stood there for an hour,
And gazed at the grand scene beneath him.

VINCENT—*Inspexit et despexit.**

        [*The Compline bell strikes, and they go in.*

    * Gazed on, and looked down upon it all.

SCENE 27.

The following is the incident which led to this Scene :—A Spirit, under the form of a Nightingale, was sent from Heaven to tell Bernard how S. Benedict was to be perfectly purified, so that when he left earth, he might go at once to Heaven. Bernard was to try his faith by a seeming violation of the most sacred of the three Vows, Obedience. Bernard, in an exquisite strain of music, expresses his willingness to obey the command, and his trust that the Abbot will be faithful to the spirit and letter of the religious rule, even unto death : and he challenges the Spirit to emulate his joy in obeying the Divine Will. The Spirit accepts the challenge, and they enter into a loving contest, which ends by the Spirit acknowledging Bernard's superiority, and falling at his feet.

Recreation-Room. — MAUR, SYLVESTER. — *Enter* CLAUDE, *just returned from a begging tour, reading a letter.*

CLAUDE (*reads aloud*)—" The buoyant gaiety of his action arrested my eye, and his song most irresistibly did my ear, as he swept round the Monastery with enthusiastic ecstasy. As he sunk at Bernard's feet, he uttered a prolonged and wonderfully beautiful cry, and then bounded aloft

with the celerity of an arrow, as if to
recover his very soul, expired in the
last elevated strain."

CLAUDE (*turns to* MAUR)—This letter came to me
from Dunstan when I was on my tour;
what does he mean, think you ? and can
I see him now ?

MAUR—No; he's in close Retreat for three next
days :
But I can tell you what he means.
He is referring to a strange contest
Which took place about a week ago,
Between Bernard and a nightingale.
Dunstan would have told you all, had not
The Abbot called him, and in his hurry to
obey,
He lost the first part of his letter: we
posted
Only what we found, the sentence you have
read.

CLAUDE—How could a bird have contest with
our Bernard ?

MAUR—I only know it had.

Dost thou remember it, Sylvester?

SYLVESTER—Remember ! can I e'er forget ?

      I thought it was an Angel

Till I stole nearer, and saw Bernard upon
    his lute

Proclaiming so bold and beautiful a challenge

That the birds flocked about him silently,

Wondering at what they heard. I wonder'd
    too.

CLAUDE—And did you hear it, Brother Maur ?

MAUR—Yes ; I was near the Abbot, who was
    standing at the recreation-window ;

His earnest eyes unoccupied with outward
    things,

      Feeding on something richer.

I lean'd and looked over, and I said :

"Father, methinks our Bernard is inspired."

" Bernard's impatient there," said he, " to
    run

Thro' his delight ; and strange it were

Thought he not, as think he may,

How every gust of music, every air,
Breathing its freshness over weary breasts,
Is a faint prelude to the Choirs above;
The Angel of Death stands in the space
     between ;
To some with invitation free and meek,
To some with flames athwart an angry brow ;
To others holds green palm and aureole
     crown,
Dreadless as is the shadow of a leaf."
And while he spoke, a sorrowing thought
Free of all gloom, o'erspread his saintly face ;
He upward looked, and sighed :
And prayed of Heaven its peace for the
     Departed.
And as he prayed, the nightingale burst
     out . . .
Oh had you heard the ravishing contention !
CLAUDE—Would that I had.
MAUR (*to* SYLVESTER)—Prithee tell him of it;
     For I must go to wait upon the Abbot.
                     [*Exit* MAUR.

SYLVESTER—Bernard could not run division
    with more art
Than did the nightingale with his various
    notes
Reply to : for a voice and glorious melody,
        It is much easier to believe
That such they were, than hope to hear
    again.
CLAUDE—How did the rivals part?
SYLVESTER—You term them rightly.
    Some time thus spent, then Bernard seem'd
        to grow
    Into a noble anger, that a bird
    Should vie with him for mastery ;
    To end the controversy, in a rapture
    Upon his instrument he plays so swiftly,
    So many voluntaries, and so quick,
    Concord in discord, lines of differing method
    Meeting in one full centre of delight.
CLAUDE—Alas ! poor nightingale.
SYLVESTER—He strove to imitate these several
        sounds :

Which when his warbling throat fail'd in,
Down dropped he at our Bernard's feet.
CLAUDE—And broke his heart—   .
    Music's first martyr ?
SYLVESTER—Not so : he only rested there a
    minute,
    Then soared aloft so high, I lost him quite
    In vortices of glory, and gold light.
CLAUDE—I've had a wondrous dream about him.
SYLVESTER—About whom ? Our Bernard ?
CLAUDE—Ay ; I thought he was an Angel, not
    a man.
    But I must not reveal it more, till GOD
    clears it.
SYLVESTER—There goes the Vesper-bell.
        [*Bell sounding for Vespers.* [*Exeunt.*

SCENE 28.

Arch-Monastery—Recreation-room.—Monks passing in and out of the room in disorder and distress: CLAUDE, DUNSTAN.

DUNSTAN (*to* CLAUDE)—You look as you had
    Seen Medusa's head ! What is the matter ?
CLAUDE—A letter has been found in Bernard's
    hand,
Offering his services to the atrocious Goth.
DUNSTAN—Does Bernard own the writing ?
CLAUDE—He says, " it is my hand : " and then
    says nothing more.
       [*Enter* SYLVESTER, FITZROI, *and* GEORGE.
SYLVESTER—Riddle upon riddle !
    I have dreamed this night Bernard was
    Clothed like innocence, all white :
    Why do I doubt ? Why do I stay demurring,
    When his guilt's so plain ?
    And yet methinks 'tis very strange,

One so devout should suddenly thus change,
And throw his nature off :
What shall I do ? shall I believe a dream ?
CLAUDE—Dreams come from GOD, full oft to
   teach us truth.
DUNSTAN—I durst venture my place in Heaven
   upon his faith.
CLAUDE—The lots of Saints are sometimes
   wrapt in
 Mysteries, and so deliver'd; such may be
   Bernard's case.
SYLVESTER—GOD grant it, Brother.
CLAUDE—I do believe his truth will soon break
   out,
 Though mountains cover it.
GEORGE—If he is guilty, what's the punishment ?
CLAUDE—Expulsion.
GEORGE—O, great GOD !
 But still I think the deep consideration
 Of what's past, more frights him,
 Than any other punishment.
DUNSTAN—Then you think he wrote the letter ?

GEORGE—I cannot tell: but why does he not
    speak?
FITZROI—To-day I met him in the Cloisters,
    By Heaven, I knew him not! until he
      bowed:
    His grief had altered so his former joyous
      being:
    What heart could see such suffering and not
      melt?
  [*Exeunt* CLAUDE, DUNSTAN, *and* GEORGE.   *Enter*
    ROMANUS.
ROMANUS—Had an Angel told it me
    The other day, I should have disbelieved.
    Oh, what a chasm in our Abbot's life hath one
      day made!
    Thus giving way with such astounding
      crash,
    Under his feet when all seemed equable,
    All hopeful, not a form of fear in sight.
    Cursed be the day, that Bernard came to us!
FITZROI—Brother, if we could see the pangs
    within

Which rend his bosom, every voice would pause
From railing and reproach.
[*Exit* FITZROI.   *Enter* AMBROSE, *a youthful Monk,*
     pale, and agitated.
AMBROSE—Can treachery be found
   Within the shadow of that lofty mien ?
   No, by the Sword of the Arch-Angel ! No.
ROMANUS—Alas ! that it should be so.
                                   [*Enter* MAUR.
ROMANUS—How fares the Abbot now ?
MAUR—I cannot penetrate the impervious gloom
   Which clouds his brow ; and only see his angel-
       smile
   Replaced by sad austerity, his tonsure blanched ;
   And his voice seldom heard : and yet
   I read his brow more agitated than severe.
ROMANUS—Oh greatest, best of human beings,
   Let not your justice be o'erpowered by your
       feelings !
MAUR—I urged for Bernard's stay.
AMBROSE—GOD bless you noble Maur !
                               [*Exit* AMBROSE.

Romanus—What! after such gross violation of
   the chief Vow?
He ought, he must be made example of—
You did not urge his stay?
Maur—Yes: else our Abbot's heart will break.
Romanus—What did the Abbot say to you?
Maur—Alas! the Abbot gave me stern rebuke;
   And said, "Then let it break, rather than
   break the Rule."
Romanus—Well might I dream last night,
   The Saints all started from their Thrones
   above,
   To stare upon the grandeur of his spirit;
   Wond'ring what new Martyr Heaven had be-
   got.
Maur—Ah, Brother! must we lose him?
Romanus—Not yet: not yet: O God forbid!
   His heart is shaken by a frightful storm;
   But he'll come through it, the purest gold
   That ever brightened in the crucible of grief.
Maur—He'll pass through it to Paradise, I
   fear.

A terror tells me so; such fearful pallor
Sits upon his face.

ROMANUS—Why should'st thou be
Surprised at this? did'st thou not mark
The ghastly hue of Ambrose's young face?
And if thou look around a pallidness
On every face is painted.

MAUR—But not like his:
He'll fight with Hell to-day.

ROMANUS—Since the cause is Thine, O LORD!
Oh, defend Thyself! defend the Rule!
Be with our Abbot in the struggle!

MAUR—And Bernard, wretched man—
Can we not pray for him?

ROMANUS—O Brother! how terrible it is to be
Scathed by that lightning which GOD's sleep-
less eye
Smites the untrue Religious: devils
Feeling it in the abysses of the abyss,
Rejoice 'twas not for them.

> [*Enter* VICTOR *hastily.*

VICTOR—The Abbot calls to Chapter.

> [*Exeunt* ROMANUS, MAUR, *and* VICTOR.

Scene 29.

Monastery Recreation-Room.—Ambrose *and* Bernard—Ambrose *ill, lies on a couch.*

———

Bernard—It is my hand, but yet I did not
    write it.
  Rather than dare to write what he forbade,
  By a slow fire I would consume this hand;
  And if I speak not truth, I should deserve to be
  Hemm'd in with a despair thicker than
  Egyptian darkness, and I a plague myself, so
  That when devils cursed beyond invention,
  To their prodigious rhetoric
  This epiphonema should be added—
  " Become as miserable as the lost Bernard!"
  Meanwhile I may not tear away the veil from
    truth,
  Or tell who wrote the letter.
Ambrose—Is Heaven alone not ignorant ?
Bernard—Oh ! that I could requite thy truth
    with confidence :

It may not be : Ambrose, why dost thou still
Persist in love so pure, yet so ungently borne?'
My claims are bankrupt; do not pledge
Friendship unto one the Abbot will
So soon dismiss.
AMBROSE—To innocence, and Heaven I trust
    your cause.
BERNARD—Were I with truth accused,
Thou should'st alone for Bernard plead.
AMBROSE—Your secresy afflicts, but cannot
    Shake my soul : I'll ask no more, if GOD
    Will not refuse to let me share your woe.
BERNARD—And die with me? for I'll soon pass
    from earth.
AMBROSE—And die with you . . .
BERNARD—Is such thy wish? then take my hand.
    O friendship, sweeter than the love of woman !
    And nearer allied to Eternity !
AMBROSE—It cannot be that you will be
    dismissed :
The Abbot comes to Chapter soon again ;
Mark well, note every look, and change,

And fix on him your searching eye, that oft
Has read his thoughts, and met his yet
Unuttered wish! then come, and give me
    hope,
And that will make me well.
BERNARD—My hope is gone to Heaven.
AMBROSE—How is the Abbot thus deceived!
  You that guard virtue, were ye asleep to
    suffer
  This mistake . . . That I show myself a
    child,
  And bewray grief in too soft a passion,
  I hope you cannot blame me.

                        [*He weeps.*

BERNARD—Weep not for me, my Brother!
  Because in death I've centred every hope—
  Only in Death . . you'll meet me there?
AMBROSE—I will.
[*Exit* BERNARD: *he goes out into the Cloister.*]
BERNARD (*alone in the Cloister.*)—'Twill soon be
    over now—
  The thought thrills me with ecstasy.

But whence this agony? Ah, GOD!
The Guardians of the human race
Pay for the honour that is done to them,
By sufferings that the other Angels
Can know nothing of..
Almighty POWER! how hast Thou made me
Capable to bear at once the extremes of
Pleasure, and of pain : Ah me! the pain now
Predominates, and will so to the end, the
Glorious issue.   O my beloved Superior!
I could weep tears of blood were I mortal,
For love of thee, for pity of myself;
O must I stab thee to the heart!—the heart?
Nay further, to the soul—
My GOD, direct and help me!
[*He passes on; goes into his Cell, and closes the*
door.

SCENE 30.

The Arch-Monastery: The ABBOT *in Chapter—*
*Monks assembled.—*BERNARD *kneels before*
the ABBOT, *who sits in deep thought.* CLAUDE
whispers to ROMANUS

CLAUDE—Good GOD ! he's grown an old man in
  two days !
ROMANUS (*shaking his fist at* BERNARD)—Curse of
  disobedience ! Thou hast made
His brow bend to the earth, sooner than
  nature.
CLAUDE—Hush, brother; let us not judge
  before the end.
[AMBROSE *rushes in haggard and trembling, and*
  throws himself before the ABBOT'S *chair.*
AMBROSE—My Lord, let Bernard stay, for he is
  innocent.
ABBOT—How dare you break the rule of Chapter
  thus ? .

Him innocent !   I heard, I saw . . .

AMBROSE *(interrupting him)*—You heard,
  You saw; Oh ! 'twas an evil vision, conjured
    up
  Against your peace, and Bernard's innocence.
  Let him remain a day.

ABBOT—No, not an hour.
  What, are you mad ?
  Leave this Assembly.   Leave it at once—
  Thy Abbot still I am, though thou forget,
  And almost seem'st to scorn to be my Son !
                              [*Exit* AMBROSE.
  Poor youth ! his grief has made him desperate.
  (Looking at BERNARD) Ah, Bernard !
  What was to me a riddle, now is plain,
  The Devil's words; pointing at you, he said
  (That day as you lay sleeping in the wood) :
  " The Abbot's heart-strings will all crack
  For this supposed Saint-Monk."

BERNARD—Speaking of me ?

ABBOT—Of you ; aye, Bernard.

BERNARD—'Twas true ; I am not what I seem :

And what you think is lost, my Vow,
I will redeem.
ABBOT—O my poor child! too safe in your
    destruction :
Sickness, and conscience desecrated,
Distract thy senses.
Could'st thou rear up another world like this,
Another like to that, and more and more,
Herein thou art most wretched; all the
    wealth
Of all those worlds could not redeem
        The loss of violated Vow.
        [*The* ABBOT *rises and turns to* MAUR.
Off with his robe, expel him from this place;
Speak for me: I can no more.
[*He sinks back in his chair, and covers his face.*
        MAUR *goes up to* BERNARD, *and stands
        before him.*
MAUR—Bernard, since by thy broken oath thou
    hast made thyself
Unworthy of that sacred Sign thou wear'st,
And of our sacred Order, into which

For former virtues we received thee first,
According to our statutes—
We here deprive thee of our habit, and
Declare thee unworthy our Society :
Using the authority the Lord Abbot
Hath given unto me, I untie this knot,
And take from thee the pleasing yoke of
    CHRIST.

                    [*Removes his Scapulaire.*
And take from off thy breast this holy Sign.
[*Takes away his cross.—The Monastery clock
    strikes.*
ABBOT (*in a very weak voice*)—Some one thank
    Heaven—I cannot.*
BERNARD—All praise be ever given !
ROMANUS—Look to the Abbot !
        See ! he faints . . .
[*The* ABBOT *falls from his chair in a swoon, and
    is carried out.*

---

* It was S. Benedict's custom to thank GOD every hour.

SCENE 31.

Arch-Monastery.— SYLVESTER *in Recreation-Room:* DUNSTAN *comes in wringing his hands.*

———

DUNSTAN—Ambrose is dying fast, and Bernard's gone.

SYLVESTER—Dying, ah! well I'm not surprised;
  I did not think his delicate physique
  could withstand such mental suffering;
  for he loved Bernard as his very soul.
  But where is Bernard gone?

DUNSTAN—No one can tell.   [*Enter* CLAUDE.

SYLVESTER—How is the Abbot?

CLAUDE—He still lies in a death-like swoon.

[*Exit* CLAUDE : *as he goes out, it thunders, and a brilliant light* appeareth above the Monastery :* DUNSTAN *and* SYLVESTER *run to the window and look up.*

* S. Benedict's departure was made known to three of his Monks in this manner:—They were returning from a Pilgrimage, and had almost reached home, when they beheld a bright pathway leading

SYLVESTER—How awful! and how beautiful!
It shooteth up to Heaven!

DUNSTAN—Ambrose is dead; I'm sure of it:
When thunder claps, Heaven likes the
tragedy;
Angels are happy when the righteous die.

SYLVESTER—Dunstan, I fear these signs point
to
A greater exit than dear Ambrose's.   Hark!
There comes a dreadful weeping from Saint
John the Baptist's Chapel.

DUNSTAN—That's where they took the Abbot.
            [*The fearful wailing becomes louder.*
What is it? . . . O Sylvester . . .

SYLVESTER (*raising his hands*)—Spare me from
ever hearing such a cry again.
            [*Enter* ROMANUS *in great agitation.*

ROMANUS—The Abbot is departed!
Soon as MAUR gave him the Viaticum,

from the Monastery, Heavenwards; and as they looked, a venerable
person asked them for whom this was prepared.   They answered
that they could not tell.   " It is the way," replied he, " that the Holy
Benedict, beloved of God, has just passed to Heaven."—*See S. Benedict's Life, by S. Gregory.*

He struggled to his feet, and throwing out
His arms cross-like, he breathed his last.
DUNSTAN—Died standing?
ROMANUS—Died standing.*
DUNSTAN—Gone without a word of Valediction.
SYLVESTER—'Twere but a mock else, for how
	could
Those he left, by any chance farewell.
Monastic life! Where is it now?
For the sun that was it's glory,
Leaves it dead in dark eclipse—
[*The cry from the Chapel is repeated.* DUNSTAN
	throws himself on his face.
SYLVESTER (*looking up and clasping his hands*)
	—O CHRIST, take pity on our misery.
ROMANUS—Come, Brothers, come!
				[*Exeunt.*

---

* A literal fact.—*See S. Gregory's Life of S. Benedict.*

SCENE 32.

Arch-Monastery.—ROMANUS *in the Cloisters.*

ROMANUS—The Rule unkept! the Offices unsung!
  Nothing save sad outcries, and speechless
      pangs—
  This grief undisciplined and desperate,
  Disgraces our Profession.
                  [*He meets* MAUR, *and walks with him.*
MAUR—How are we forsaken! What have we
      lost!
  He was the vision of a Heaven unto us—
  With virtues thick as frosty night with stars;
  And all the motions of his mind celestial!
  Romanus, what are all our lives and actions,
  But counterfeits in arras to his worth.
ROMANUS—Forgive me, my Superior, if I say,
  Your grief makes you forget your duty:
  Be pleased to call to mind his last will and
      testament,
  Written with his own hand, that you should
  Take his place, and faithfully keep Rule.

Will you, O Maur ! leave anything that he
Desired ungranted ? Need I say more ?
We cannot reach his goodness, yet we may
Reach constantly to something that is near it.
O goodness unsurpassed, stand to Eternity
For all good Monks to imitate !

MAUR—Ah, Brother, all that I am's not worth
    a hair from him !
Thanks, thanks, for your reproof ;
It's roused me from my selfish sorrow.
I will not leave his wish unsatisfied,
If all that's left in me can answer it.

ROMANUS—I've only this to add ;
    I ask you in the Brethren's name, to take
The Abbot's office.   Full well knew Nature,
Thou wert fitter far to be a Ruler
O'er us than a Brother : which henceforth be !
The Brothers all await your answer.

MAUR—Tell them to meet me in the Chapel.

[*Exit* ROMANUS. MAUR *enters the Chapel and kneels*
    before the Altar. Enter Brothers ROMANUS,
    CLAUDE, DUNSTAN, VICTOR, GEORGE, FITZROI,
    JAMES, JOHN, SYLVESTER, CUTHBERT, SE-

BASTIAN, *and others.   They all kneel in silence for a time.*

*   *   *   *   *   *

MAUR—Look down, look down !
Cœlitum excelsissimum !
Benedict ! hear the sacred Vow I make—
One moment cease to gaze on perfect bliss,
And bend thy glorious eyes to earth and me;
(O blessed eyes ! how nobly shone your com-
    forts !
They shine for Angels now).
Brothers departed ! if you have arrived
Through all impediments of purging fire,
To that bright Heaven, where our Abbot
    reigns,
Behold ye also, and attend my Vow—
If ever I do yield, or give consent, .
By any action, word, or thought to break
Our Rule inspired, may then just Heaven
    shower down
Unheard of curses on me : and now,
                                        [*Rising up.*

My heart has some relief, having thus far,
Discharged this debt, incumbent on my love.
ROMANUS — Yet one thing more we would engage
    from thee—
Be consecrated Abbot, and without delay.
Come to the Minster and repeat this vow.
MAUR—I will attend you.   [*Exeunt.*

SCENE 33.

THE ANGELS, LUCIAN, *and* BERNARD.

LUCIAN—Well Bernard, it is finished!
BERNARD—And gloriously :
  Did you mark these eager spirits flashing on
    to pay their homage to Saint Benedict?
LUCIAN—I did; and some of them I recognised.
BERNARD—Yes; you must have seen
  Eutropius, Scholastique, Adele, Angela, Dora,
    Placidus, Evangeline, William, Richard,
    Vincent, and Ambrose, and many, many
    others.

LUCIAN—And some were there before their
   time. I wondered how they came.
BERNARD—I'll tell you how and why :
   CHRIST was so pleased and touched with the
      dear Monks' obedience and heart-stricken
      resignation, that when good Maur was
      consecrated Abbot, He let a trance con-
      vey them all up to the Palace of the
      Highest Heaven, to comfort and sustain
      their future life on earth : and oh ! their
      rapture when they saw Saint Benedict !
LUCIAN—Hark, brother, hark !
   There is a hurricane of blissfulness on High !
BERNARD—'Tis Heaven rising from ten thou-
      sand thrones, to entertain divine Saint
      Benedict.
LUCIAN—Hark, hark again !
   The sun-eyed Seraphs hail him !
BERNARD—Come Lucian, let us join that har-
      mony Seraphic, and do him reverence,
      whom GOD delights to honour.
                              [*Exeunt.*

                    FINIS.

www.ingramcontent.com/pod-product-compliance
Lightning Source LLC
Chambersburg PA
CBHW030542040726
47497CB00008B/2555